BLOOD OF THE LOST

THE HUNTER GAMES

BOOK TWO

ARIEL DAWN

NAUGHTY NIGHTS PRESS LLC • CANADA

Blood Of The Lost

The Hunter Games

Book Two

Copyright ©2023 Ariel Dawn

ISBN: 978-1-77357-557-5

978-1-77357-556-8

Naughty Nights Press LLC

Cover Design by Willsin Rowe

BLOOD OF THE LOST

Immense heartbreak. A deadly fight. A new beginning.

Jake Dallas has lived for nothing but the hunt for years. After losing his wife and child, he swore he'd never let anyone into his heart again. When a routine monster hunt turns deadly, Jake is given a second chance at life... as one of the same beasts he hunted.

Four years ago, Midnight was attacked and left for dead. All she's desired since that life-changing day is to find the ones who took her daughter and rescue her. That is until she saves a handsome, hunter-turned monster who might just be the answer to her dark prayers.

Will Dallas be able to put aside a life of slaying and heartache to rescue a lost child?
Or will old habits die hard and force him to choose sides?

Grief is the price we pay for love.
-Queen Elizabeth II

It doesn't matter what you are, it only matters what you do.
It's your choice.
-Sam Winchester, Supernatural

1

THE AIR WAS thick with broken promises, tainted memories, and the scent of blood. The sounds of Ava's screams would haunt Dallas for the rest of his undead life.

Because as Dallas lay motionless on the blood-soaked ground of the Marquis, suspended in motion between life and death, he could feel his insides hardening, changing.

Like a moth inside a cocoon, all he could do was wait for the transition to take hold.

"Get up," the sound of a woman's voice called to him, but he did not recognize it.

Dallas tried to move his fingers, his toes, but everything felt heavy.

He grunted in response as his eyelashes fluttered. The room he was in was dark, the only light the bright flash from a phone screen.

"Fucking shut that off," he growled, stretching his fingers. He moved his hand to shield his eyes. The light was so bright, blinding almost.

"Oh, this one's got spunk," another woman's voice carried excitedly.

"Who do you think is responsible for making him?"

ARIEL DAWN

Dallas attempted to move his legs, the effort nearly exhausting.

His entire body felt as if he'd been hit by a freight train. He held his hand in front of his eyes, noting the mess of blood all over his skin.

Memories filtered back into his brain.

The Djinn heading for Ava and Mal.

How he'd pushed them out of the way without a second thought.

There had been so much blood...

Dallas ran his hands over his chest, feeling for the gaping wound he knew should be there. But he felt no such thing, just cold, congealed blood, and soft, sore skin among the shredded remains of his costume.

"Can you get up?"

Dallas's gaze settled on one of the women, the one with the excited voice.

She kneeled before him, long raven waves falling over her shoulders. Her pale skin and glowing aquamarine eyes were indicative of her breed of monster.

Djinn.

She looked strangely familiar...

Dallas leaned in close to the Djinn, letting her scent fill his airways. She smelled of woods and citrus mixed with vanilla cake batter, and he could feel her natural siren aura trying to capture him.

"You got a name, sweetheart, or should I just call you mine?" he asked, the words empty, soulless. It wasn't anything he hadn't done before, but this time... it felt different.

Because there was only one woman he wanted to call his, and he'd left her with the vampire who'd claimed her blood...

The Djinn giggled.

Fucking giggled like an innocent child.

"You can call me—"

"Midnight?" Her name came to him without warning as the memories flooded him.

"Oh! You're the guy from the bar... the... hunter ..." she said as her eyes widened in surprise.

"He's a hunter?" The other woman shrieked, and Dallas's gaze was pulled away. The other Djinn resembled Midnight, though she was taller with short chin length black hair that boasted bright blue streaks.

"Ami will have a field day with him..."

Midnight pursed her lips as she set her hand on his shoulder, imploring him with her gaze.

"Perhaps he could be of use to us... to

Ami," Midnight said as she tugged Dallas's sleeve.

"Can you get up?" she asked again, her voice soft.

Dallas wiggled his toes in his boots, bending his legs and knees slowly. They still ached, but feeling had come back. He motioned forward, getting up too fast as he started to feel dizzy.

"I'm fine..." he bit, shaking off the touch of the sweet-voiced Djinn.

He could hear the sounds of sirens in the distance, and he knew they were right. He did need to move.

He needed to find Malcolm, Ava...

The thought of the Crowleys caused an ache in his heart as his stomach twisted in nauseous knots.

He was starving. He grabbed his stomach, a painful growl escaping his throat.

"What the fuck..."

"He needs to eat," Midnight protested.

"The damn police will be here any minute, Midnight!" the other one bit out.

Dallas jumped as Midnight slid her hand in his, tugging him toward her.

"Whoever made him doesn't look like they're coming back. He's one of us now, Rebel. I won't leave him to the fucking *wolves*."

Dallas tried to make sense of her words, but he couldn't. His head was pounding, his body aching, and he was *starving*. His gaze fell on the short vixen in front of him, his mouth going dry.

I wish...

The sound of doors opening, of rushed footsteps, told them all they needed to know.

And so Jake Dallas followed the Djinn into the shadows, escaping into the night.

2

MIDNIGHT'S SHOULDERS SANK as she caught up to Rebel. The lumbering hunter walked behind them, keeping a safe distance.

As he should, waking up to find out you're not dead doesn't always go down so smoothly.

"This is a royally bad idea, you know. Djinn or not, he's a fucking hunter. Hunters can't be trusted," Rebel said, casting her a suspicious look.

"Yeah, a hunter that was left for dead by his fellow hunters."

"You don't know that they won't come back for him. We don't need that kind of danger. It's reckless, even for you."

"Hunters also have experience *hunting* down monsters, Reby," Midnight whispered, her gaze dropping to the freshly turned Djinn behind her.

"He was hunting us, Midnight. The Heartsgrave, and Ami..." Rebel whispered, her tone worried.

She knew Rebel was right. The decision to rescue Dallas, the hunter in their midst, was impulsive, and it was certainly reckless. But Midnight couldn't help but feel some sense of magnetism, of universal understanding. She knew it didn't make any sense, but her gut never lied to her. After she'd met her supposed bitter end, she learned to listen to it.

But Midnight had tried everything else. Amora, or as she preferred to be called, Ami, had promised her resources. She had promised her a chance at the Boracellis, the vampires who'd stolen everything from her. Ami had promised her the resources she needed to survive, to find her daughter, in exchange for a little loyalty, and blood.

For Midnight, it was a small price to pay.

Ami had built her little army of Djinn and ghouls from the ground up, promising revenge and justice against those who had wronged them, preying on the desperation of newly turned or lost individuals who had nothing else to lose.

Dangle life in front of a dying man, and you'd be surprised what they would do for just one more day.

And then one day turns into one hundred, until the blood and the chase is all you know.

But Midnight was tired of running, tired of chasing leads on her own with The Heartsgrave that ended up being nothing but cold, dead ends. She was tired of unearthing empty graves.

It seemed as if every time they thought they'd found a lead, or an answer, they'd only found more questions, and they kept getting further and further away.

"Where the fuck are we going?" Dallas grumbled behind her.

"To base," Midnight said.

"Ya'll don't have a car or..."

"Our motorcycles are just a little while away," she answered as Rebel smacked her arm, casting her glare.

"Motorcycles, huh? Didn't peg you for biker babes."

"You don't get to peg us for anything, *hunter*," Rebel bit.

Dallas growled, the sound vibrating deep within Midnight's chest, striking a chord and causing literal hairs to stand on her skin.

Well, that's new...

Though a part of her had to admit, she was intrigued by such a visceral reaction. She hadn't remembered feeling quite so affected when they'd met the other night... when he was a human.

She knew then he was a hunter, and she'd been intrigued. Though she'd been around as a Djinn long enough to pick up on desires and wishes without needing to concentrate too much. The night he'd sequestered her, likely for his own gain, for information, she'd felt a wave of desire and pain from the man. He didn't *want* to hurt her.

But if push came to shove he would do whatever was needed to get the answers *he* sought, even if it meant killing her. She could feel his disdain and his vengeance, thick like smog in his aura. And that sort of focus, that sort of dedication to the job was what she needed to find Emma.

Because wherever her daughter was, she knew she wasn't safe, and if push came to shove, she needed someone who wouldn't blink an eye at putting a few monsters in the ground if that was what it took to get her back.

Midnight needed a hunter like Jake Dallas.

When they'd finally come to the clearing, Midnight could breathe.

"The Clam is about fifteen minutes away," she said as she swung her legs over the seat.

"I'm driving," he said with stern command.

Midnight turned to look up at the lumbering man, his blue eyes vibrant against his skin. She remembered appreciating their beauty when he was a human, when he'd had her trapped against the wall, lighting up her insides like a fire with just his gaze, all that anger festering below his surface, but... Rimmed with that ever-present aqua glow that was part of his DNA now, she couldn't help but suck in a breath. They were cold, icy, but yet wondrously captivating, and Midnight had to remind herself to breathe. For under the fiery gaze of this newborn monster, she felt frozen.

Get a hold of yourself!

It's just the Djinn DNA doing what it was made to do.

She shook the odd thoughts off, setting a hand on her hip as she looked up at him. "Um, this is *my* ride, so I make the rules," she said with a smirk.

Dallas looked at her as if she'd grown two heads.

"You can ride behind me or you can walk. Your choice," she said as she turned away from him, turning the ignition on.

"You've got to be kidding me," he quipped. "I'd crush you."

Midnight cast him a rueful smile. "I can handle more than you think. Perks of being a well-fed Djinn."

Dallas only rolled his eyes, his jaw tensing.

A Djinn's strength came not just from their supernatural DNA, but from the energy they consumed. Midnight, Rebel, Enchantress... most of the Djinn in The Heartsgrave had pulled more than their weight to bring in a boatload of humans for both the party and to be the spots— the proverbial horses Ami's vampire investors purchased for both betting and consumption—and until the whole place erupted in chaos, Midnight and Rebel had relished in the all you could consume buffet of desire and wishful thinking. She'd consumed enough wishes that she felt as if she could, in fact, take on a man the size of Dallas if she wanted to.

Instinctively, Midnight wanted to protest, but when she looked at Dallas underneath the pale moonlight, his costume torn to shreds, stained with blood, his bright eyes imploring hers, resistance was futile. Because she understood what it meant to be thrown into a world you didn't understand, to wake up as someone you didn't know anymore, and so her gaze and voice softened.

"I know this is a lot to process, believe me," she said, remembering the moment Ami had found her, how she'd struggled to breathe. She was terrified, unaware of everything that had truly transpired. Her gut told her she could trust the woman who held her, who counted to ten, coaching her to take deep breaths until her breath had stabilized.

"I've been there. But I promise, you can trust me," she said as he looked over her shoulder.

Dallas crossed his arms, and she noted his muscles as he did so.

He really will make a formidable Djinn...

She waited for him to concede.

Dallas only looked at her with anger and pain, clearly waging a war within himself. To trust or not to trust.

What would a hunter do?

"Fine. I'll walk," he said.

Midnight couldn't help but let out a laugh.

"You don't even know where the Clam is," she said with amusement.

"I'll figure it out," he said stubbornly.

"And you don't know the first thing about being a newborn Djinn." Rebel scoffed, taking off ahead of her, clearly not entertaining Dallas's attitude or her friend's impulsiveness.

Though Midnight couldn't really blame her. She knew plenty of men like Dallas when she'd been alive. Men who always had a way of getting under her skin. Stubborn, arrogant, and remiss to admit when they were out of their element, who would rather walk in circles than take help from a stranger.

Especially a woman.

Perhaps if her ex, Trevor, had listened to her, perhaps if they would have been able to see eye to eye... she would not have wound up a Djinn, he would not have wound up dead, and her daughter would not have ended up in the hands of the real monsters.

The Boracellis.

When Dallas turned heel, walking in the direction Rebel had taken off, he did not speak. He only slid his large hands in his pants pocket, standing in the moonlight looking every bit like a bloodied Phantom of the Opera. His dark hair was disheveled, his aquamarine eyes like stars in the night sky, his costume tattered and bloody, and he wore a look on his face that made every hair on Midnight's body stand on end.

There was no denying that hunter or monster, this man was dangerous, and she needed to remember that.

"Suit yourself," she said with a laugh, as she sped off with lightning speed toward the Drowned Clam, toward the

call of wishes, dreams, and sweet, sweet
blood.

3

DALLAS BIT HIS tongue. When Midnight and her pain in the ass friend had taken off, he could finally think.

He slid his hand in his pocket, pulling out his phone. It was smashed beyond belief, and he could barely read the screen. Not to mention the battery life looked to be about ten percent.

"Fuck," he said with a grumble as he slid it back in his pocket.

He paced back and forth, his stomach roiling with nausea from the onslaught of everything.

The need to contact Malcolm, or even Ava, was prevalent, but could he trust them?

He'd certainly trusted the Crowley's before he'd...

Died.

Dallas swallowed as the memory of death engulfed him. The pain of the open wound that the Djinn woman, Enchantress, had ripped in his chest, the cold that seeped through his body as he bled out. The images that flashed in his mind like a highlight reel of his life.

Running down the football field in high school and college.

Dancing with Laura at their tiny firehall wedding.

ARIEL DAWN

The first appointment where he'd heard his daughter's heartbeat, terrified and overjoyed at the same time.

The day he'd come home to find out Laura had been killed, when he saw the bite marks on her throat, on her stomach, and thighs.

The day he killed his first vampire.

All the endless gigs and laughs he'd shared with Malcolm and the hunters they'd picked up along their travels, Vinny, Tito, and even Hunter.

The moment he'd seen Ava's bite mark and how it sent him spiraling.

Holding Ava when he was afraid of falling in love again.

Everything meshed together into one conglomerate of pain and despair as the memory of Ava's tears streaming down her face, as her brother grabbed her, pulsed through him like a heartbeat all its own, mixed with the things that would never be.

Things he'd only dreamed of, wished of at the precipice of death because he'd never given in to such things for fear he'd lose them again.

And as death called him, as he lay bleeding on the concrete floor of a massacre at the Marquis, Dallas lost himself in those hopes and dreams. The what if's he'd kept buried deep.

What his daughter would have looked like.

What he would have done if blood hadn't stained his hands and took his innocence.

In death, Dallas dreamed of a life he'd never gotten the chance to have, and for the absolute bliss of a single moment, he'd lived it.

Then he was awakened by a bright light, and not that of the one most people wish to see. Dallas was awakened by a blinding flashlight, and voices that belonged to creatures who certainly were not angels.

Dallas walked with hurried pace along the road, arms crossed as he chewed on the facts he did have.

I saved Mal and Ava.

The Djinn fucking bit me, and died.

I died.

But their venom reanimated me, and turned me into a damn monster, what are the fucking odds?

He knew one bite alone could turn a human, but it was unlikely. The lore spoke of the Djinn needing to feed on dreams and wishes, and for a full bonding, or "rebirth" as they called it, he would have needed to drink the blood of the Djinn that bit him to become a fully fledged monster... which he hadn't.

Because Malcolm *killed* the monster who'd attacked him.

Because Ava and Mal kill monsters, it's what they do.

But would they really kill me?

The fact Dallas could not answer *no* to the question of whether or not his allies would not kill him on sight, especially because he was no longer—human—entirely made him want to throw up.

Maybe they could help me find some way out of this...

His head was spinning. He wracked his brain for something, anything he could remember about what Hunter had told him over the years about the Djinn.

If the situation were reversed, and it was Mal or Ava who'd awakened as a monster, would he put them six feet under?

Dallas's stomach roiled with hunger and disgust, for he knew the answer.

Being a hunter wasn't for the faint of heart. It meant seeing and knowing things no one else did, and often times, it meant doing things no one should ever want to do.

Including killing your closest friends when they turn into the enemy.

He huffed out a frustrated sigh. Nothing made sense, and another wave of nausea hit him. The night air was cool to the touch, and Dallas welcomed it against the heat of his skin.

Think, D, think. You know there's got

to be a way out of this, and not one that ends with you in the ground. You can fix this... somehow. There's got to be a spell or a cure, or some way to reverse what's been done...

As he walked, he poured over the night's happenings in his mind, but the hunger inside of him was starting to feel painful and he was no closer to answering the burning questions that plagued him.

And he knew it was only wishful thinking. The lore had never spoken of an antidote, or even a spell to break the Djinn curse.

But that doesn't mean there isn't a way...

In the distance he could see the light of the Drowned Clam, where he'd been only a day or so ago...

Where he'd met Midnight, for the first time. He'd been there on a mission, pressed to dig up intel on the vampire who controlled the Clam's operations, who was the one in charge of the Marquis's masquerade and who planned to host a free for all human buffet.

It wasn't uncommon for supernaturals to align if they had a common interest, after all, monsters were innately selfish creatures. Alliances were hard to come by with vampires though, being as it seemed to be well known knowledge that even among monsters, the bloodsuckers were sorely despised due to their cockroach ability to remain at the top of the monster food chain.

They were natural enemies of everyone, so what reason would the

Djinn have to align with them?

Vampires and Djinn were not the only creatures capable of luring prey. He'd played his part then, in the Drowned Clam. Dallas had long been trapping female monsters in his web for information, as well as to kill them, and therefore, he was certainly a pro at turning on his charm, eliciting his sex appeal and dominance to get whatever intel he and his fellow hunters needed.

But that had been before Ava and Cassius had arrived and distracted him.

The sight of Ava so close to the vampire who'd marked her lit his blood on fire. Despite her reassurances, she was far too close to the bloodsucker for his liking. It was almost as if she *trusted* him, and Dallas was appalled at the idea that anyone could trust a literal monster.

Especially Ava.

Ava...

The memory of her eyes wide with terror would be tattooed on his soul forever, and his heart ached as reality punched him in the stomach again.

He knew as bad as he wanted to run to her and hold her in his arms, tell her he was fine... that somehow they could fix this... he wasn't fine.

And while he refused to give up hope that there was a way of fixing his predicament, he knew doing such a thing would only put her in danger. He hadn't yet grasped everything, but the hunger inside of him, the heightened sound in his ears, and the sudden clarity in his sight were indicative enough that he was now a predatory creature, and not a man.

Because he was a monster now, and not even he was capable of understanding what that meant at the moment, as his hunger gnawed at him, the need to *consume* hope, dreams, and wishes, to touch and anchor himself to the energy that flowed from within was so overwhelming. And if there was one thing Dallas didn't want, it was to endanger the woman he'd fallen in love with... despite the fact he knew she didn't love him. Even the thought of her made his heart ache, because he knew he could not trust himself to not touch her everywhere, to not *feed* on the hopes and dreams of the prettier Crowley, even if they didn't include him.

He'd thought they'd had more time. That in time, maybe Ava could have learned to truly love him, and that maybe one day free from her mark, they could have built something together from the ashes of the blood they'd lost.

Anger and remorse festered along with guilt and frustration in his blood, and he could feel his pulse racing. Monsters had taken everything from him. His wife and unborn child, his ignorance, Mal and his fellow hunters... even the glimmer of a future with Ava.

The fury inside Dallas festered like an unbridled hurricane, begging to be set free as he tried to regain his thoughts. He needed to think clearly. Like Malcolm always did when they were in sticky situations.

And he'd been in plenty of ill-fated situations before, which he had escaped within an inch of his life, so surely a solution of some kind would present itself, if he could just think clearly...

He made it to the parking lot before he got a heady whiff of... *desire.*

Desire mixed with sadness and longing, and *hope.*

He turned his head instantly to find a long-legged blonde stumbling across the parking lot to her car. The world around him got smaller, the air thinner, as his gaze fixed on her. Every muscle in his body tightened and his blood rushed. Drawn by his natural inclinations toward trouble, he moved to stop her, somehow jumping mere feet in seconds like he'd just... transported from one place to another solely by *thinking* about it.

Yeah, that's definitely new.

The prevalent need in him to save

this woman was an override, and he'd fully intended to perhaps drive this woman home, because he knew she was drunk and it was the right thing to do.

Jake Dallas had always prided himself on doing the right thing, even when it wasn't the easiest thing.

"Give me your keys," he said the words commandingly, like he would have normally, but something about the way they sounded in the air, he couldn't deny they carried a tone that was... mysterious. Intoxicating, even to his own ears.

The woman shoved him, telling him to 'fuck off, fucker,' and he pursed his lips.

"You're in no state to drive," he said, grabbing for her keys himself.

"And who the fuck you think you are?

My knight in shining armor? Fuck off," she bit, her anger, her emotion boiling to the surface.

He could practically taste the fury, like cinnamon bubblegum.

Hot, mouthwatering.

Her voice echoed in his brain, like an array of whispers. He could hear it even though she didn't speak, as she looked at him with fire in her eyes. Longing, sadness, anger... desire... all of it mixed together like some heady cocktail, tinged with the scent of pineapples and coconuts so prominent, he wondered if she'd *taste* like a margarita.

She smelled *delicious*.

Dallas stumbled back himself, feeling a deep, burning need to *consume*. To give this women exactly what she *needed*.

What she *wished* for.

"No," he said, but he wasn't sure who was referring to. His muscles strained, his feet dragging on the pavement as he fought to move away, but like a magnet, he couldn't separate from what was now his nature.

Dallas grabbed at her keys with precision, his fingertips curling around her wrist, and she struggled against him.

"Get off of me," she said as she brought her knee up, aiming for his groin, but she missed.

His eyes held her in place, and he could feel his blood heating, could feel his stomach *opening* up, ready for its feast. Powerless to the new, magnetic feeling, he opened his mouth to speak, but instead only fangs shoved through his gums, and the woman whimpered in his grasp.

"Please, let me go," she whined.

In his mind he knew how Djinn fed. Like vampires, like demons and incubi, they consumed blood.

Human blood.

But it was more or less what was *in* the blood that they hungered for. According to the lore, human blood carried more than just cells. It carried their hopes, dreams, and their *wishes.*

And as Dallas tightened his grip on the woman in front of him, as her fear ebbed off of her, her cheeks flushed.

Dallas wanted to let her go. He truly did, but he wasn't in control anymore. The monster inside of him was, and he did not want to let such a delicious morsel go to waste.

"I'm so fucking sorry about this," he said as a mixture of guilt, shame, and remorse came over him.

"God, please forgive me," he said as she dropped her keys to the ground.

The taste of blood wasn't as pungent as he thought it would be, but it wasn't the blood that tore him apart from the inside.

It was the *taste* of her desire, her dreams, her wishes. Her world crashed through him, like a highlight reel as the warm, sweet blood coursed down his throat. The relief that overcame him was sinful, sweet, and wonderfully fulfilling.

Dallas knew *how* the Djinn prayed on their victims. He knew they preyed on hopes, dreams, and wishes, but until that very moment, he hadn't known truly what that meant.

BLOOD OF THE LOST

He could see her memories, her dreams, like a movie in his own head. How she longed for a man who didn't belong to her and how she wanted nothing more than to be his everything. This man who had a life, a family. Her desire, her *hope*, her wishful thinking was sweeter than a birthday cake as he drank down the blood, as her energy wrapped around him like a cozy blanket, warming him all throughout. For it was the passion, the love in those thoughts, no matter how depraved and haunting they were for someone who clearly didn't reciprocate such things.

Who took advantage of her in the dark, shadowed space of his office when he'd told his wife he needed to work late.

The image of the woman in his arms beneath the undeserving man, breasts on full display, caused his cock to twitch, as lust formed in his being; no doubt a side affect from the lust filled wishes and desires of the woman in his arms.

Dallas's eyes fluttered open as his sight cleared and he watched the color drain from her eyes. He knew he needed to stop, but he'd never felt so ignited, so weightless and euphoric in all his life. Dead or alive.

"Georgie, please... I want to hear you say it," she cried, her face going pale, but her expression soft and full of longing. She reached out her fingers, running the tips of her nails down his heated skin. The touch felt just as overwhelming as the taste of blood, and he was powerless to fight the desire culminating inside of him.

In the years following his wife's loss, before he'd crossed the line with Ava, Dallas had more than taken his share of one night stands. Like Mal's need to drink to forget about all that rested on his shoulders, Dallas lost himself in nameless women in blurred towns, if only to forget that he'd loved and lost.

The woman groaned in response as her back thudded against the car and Dallas clutched her body to his as he turned her around, her back against the car door. She wrapped her leg around him, pulling him closer, dragging her nails over his chest through his tattered shirt. Her dress rode up her thighs and instinct took over, though Dallas wasn't sure which instinct it truly was. His own, or the newfound monster who was hijacking his brain. On either account, he couldn't deny the need, the hunger he felt to take what was being offered to him, because her desire tasted sweet, but the promise of forgetting all that haunted him was too difficult to fight, and he wanted to forget.

He wanted to forget about Malcolm and Ava, and Laura, and his friends, the life he should have had. He wanted to forget the pain of dying, and the terror of waking up to find he was the one thing he'd never wished to be. A monster.

Dallas ran his hands over her thighs, his fingertips gripping her flesh with ferocity as blood coated his throat, sweet desire and hope filling him, sating his hunger all the while making it feel as if he would never get enough. His cock twitched as the woman in his grasp writhed beneath him, touching him, grasping at him as she begged for *Georgie* to tell her he loved her. Something the ass had never done, apparently.

And something about that realization, that he could see her memories, sift through her thoughts and that they, too, filled him with desire and hunger, pulled Dallas back from the ledge.

She didn't want *him.*

She wanted the man she loved, some asshole who didn't deserve her or the way she willingly gave herself to him.

He dropped her like a hot potato as he backed away, whispering no to the wind.

The woman fell to the ground, and he backed up right into something solid, no someone... someone smaller, but just as real as he was.

"I tried to tell you," the voice said calmly.

Dallas turned to see familiar eyes, a short, smirking Midnight behind him. She casually strolled toward where the woman lay on the ground, trying to catch her breath.

Dallas couldn't tear his eyes away from her and she looked around, confused and desperate.

"Georgie..." she called out, reaching for the air. "Gerogie where are you, where did you go—"

Midnight cradled the woman in her arms, brushing her hair back gently with a touch that seemed far too caring for a monster. Dallas could only watch, frozen in despair, his mind now void of the woman's sweet voice, the taste of blood on his tongue still lingering and his cock throbbing in his pants.

Midnight plucked the keys from the ground, unlocked the car, and helped the woman in the backseat.

"Georgie wants you to get some rest, sweetheart," Midnight said, her voice full of mystery and intrigue, tinged with the same command Dallas had when he spoke.

He could feel an innate desire to answer her call, even though it wasn't directed at him.

Dallas was frozen in place by his own remorse, his own terror, and the hard, cold truth.

He was well and truly a monster now.

Midnight sauntered slowly over to him, appraising him with concern. She stood in front of him, coming up barely to just below his chest, exactly where his double star tattoos lay.

"Is she..."

"She'll be fine. Just needs to sleep off the drain."

"Drain?" Dallas's voice cracked at the words. Midnight looked at him with kind, understanding eyes and he hated it.

Empathy from a monster was like a cold splash of water.

"Judging by her palor, and the fact she's alive, I'd say she'll recover quickly, unless..." Midnight chewed her lip. "Did she say I wish?" she asked.

Dallas shook his head. "No."

What did that have to do with anything?

"Wishful thoughts hold a lot of power," she said softly. "It's why they taste so good. If someone says those two words, they're giving you everything. The power to grant that wish comes at a cost most humans don't understand."

She reached out slowly, cautiously, brushing some blood from his face, from the corner of his lips. He instantly recoiled from her gentle touch, feeling the shame wrack him as his stomach settled and his cock twitched.

"This isn't who I am," he bit as he swatted her hand away.

"It is now," she said as she dropped her hand.

"I'm not some fucking monster genie who hurts people by exploiting their inner most hopes and fears—"

Midnight grabbed his hand anyway, despite his sudden reaction. This time he did not push her away, as she implored his gaze with a softness that called to his aching heart. Something told him it was okay, that he could trust this woman, but he had no reason to believe such things.

After all, he barely knew her.

"I didn't drink from the Djinn that bit me," he said as he racked his brain.

He had thought perhaps there was a slim chance this... situation... would be like the time Tito was bit by a chucacabra. He'd taken on some qualities, some side effects from the bite, but they'd worn off with the right antidote, which had worked because Tito hadn't bitten anyone, hadn't hunted or fed on anyone before receiving the antidote.

"I'm not..."

Midnight sighed. "You think because you didn't bond to the Djinn that bit you, that somehow you are free? That you are not what you are." Her words were solid, an unwavering statement.

"I am not a monster," Dallas said, but he could hear the sour pitch of his voice and the contempt in the lie.

He only chose not to believe it.

Sane humans didn't go around biting people, drinking their blood, hearing their thoughts and being turned on in the process.

Midnight brushed her thumb over his knuckles, her touch sending little jolts of electricity through his veins. His cock twitched, and his heart raced, but he wasn't entirely sure it wasn't just the euphoria of what had happened causing such a visceral reaction.

Though the hunger was still there, wanting more of the sweet taste of hopes and dreams, wishing for blood, energy, and flesh to sate it once more.

"Come on. We need to get you some fresh clothes, get you cleaned up. Plus, there's someone I'd like you to meet."

Dallas looked down at himself, noting his tattered Phantom of the Opera costume was barely hanging on by a thread, and his pants were covered in blood and dirt. A part of him knew that whatever his next step was, Midnight was right on one account. He did need to get cleaned up, he needed to get back to a sense of normalcy so that perhaps he could deal with this... situation... head on. He'd never thought himself capable of such things. After all, he helped people, saved people.

But right now, I need to save myself.

Before it's too late.

And so Dallas followed Midnight into the Drowned Clam like a lamb to the slaughter. He was numb, frozen by this new reality, from what had just happened, but if there was one thing Dallas knew how to do, it was fight, and he knew the fight for himself, for his life had only just begun.

Because as he let her pull him through the night, through the thick crowd of humans with their *incessant* inner chatter rattling in his head, he knew there was no going back to the way things were.

Not now that he'd tasted hope, dreams, and wishes, not now that he'd crossed the line into becoming the very thing he hated.

4

THIS IS BAD.

This is very, very bad.

Malcolm huffed as he threw the keys on the end table in Dallas's foyer.

Well, technically it's my foyer, now, I guess.

It had been over a week since his best friend slash partner Jake Dallas's 'death.'

Though the term death would imply

that Dallas had gone the way most hunters did, biting the proverbial supernatural bullet and going to the good place.

For better or for worse, Malcolm Crowley was experienced in the aftermath of death, having buried his parents, and several hunter acquaintances from supernatural circumstances.

But not once had he come back for a body that was not to be found.

He'd gone over the moment in his head plenty of times. He'd seen the light leave Dallas's eyes, heard as his friend called out that he saw his deceased wife and daughter as he undoubtedly saw 'the light.'

Yet when he'd gone back to collect Dallas's body for the hunter's pyre, to burn both in remembrance and to prevent supernatural mishaps, there had been no body to haul.

Which means I was too late...

It was as if he had completely disintegrated into the charred remains of the Marquis, but Malcolm knew better.

Mal settled on Dallas's couch, feeling a bit worse for wear. The house was seemingly untouched, which told him wherever his former partner had gone, he hadn't come home while Malcolm had been pretending everything was fine back in Chester with the rest of the crew, including Ava.

It had taken nearly everything in Malcolm to look at his sister and lie to her.

Again.

First with our parents, then with my

leaving... and now...

He'd wanted so badly to tell her the truth, that somewhere, somehow... Dallas was out there. But he knew he wasn't *alive.* Well, not in the sense that he and Ava were alive, with warm blood and alcohol running through their veins.

Mal felt his stomach twist in agony, as the memory of the Djinn's fangs tearing into Dallas's skin forced its way through, mingling with the memory of the metallic scent of blood hanging in the air.

Of Jake Dallas's blood smeared across Ava's shimmering white dress, and the way he touched her face, looked into her eyes.

How he'd called her...'kitten'.

Malcolm thought he'd imagined it. People often hallucinated or made up things to cope with trauma, especially in dire situations such as fighting monsters in a darkened basement of a building owned by vampires. After all, there were no secrets between him and his partner. At least, that was what he had thought.

Secrets were a dime a dozen with his sister, but that was only because she was the only family he had left. He needed to protect her, to keep her safe...

There wasn't enough time to dredge up all the bloody details of when his sister and friend had decided to fuck him over, and there was certainly no point in throwing salt on such a fresh, guttural wound now, and certainly not at the time the man lay dying in her arms.

Telling Ava that Dallas may be alive would surely compromise any mission he had to find his partner and do what *needed* to be done. Ava was too close to the fire, and now that he knew the truth, he knew ultimately involving her would put them both in danger. Because for better or worse, he and his sister were cut from the same cloth, and Ava was like a dog with a bone. When she had her sights set on something, there was no negotiating, and Malcolm knew better than anyone how emotion clouded judgment. He'd spend more than a decade steeling his resolve to stay on task, to avoid emotion and attachment, for this very reason.

And then I met Cleo...

He wished to dispel all thoughts of the omega wolf from his mind, the woman he'd met two years prior. Who claimed he was her *mate...* Who he'd called in a drunken state to cry to when he thought he'd lost his best friend...

Malcolm also knew, without a doubt that if Dallas was not six feet under, he was a monster, and he'd have to kill him. Family or not.

He thought back to the first year on the road he'd spent with Dallas, to the endless nights spent in his candy apple red Chevelle eating junk food and singing along to the various rock stations to pass the time, before they'd met Vinny, Tito, and Hunter. Before they'd started their band, Blood Of My Enemy.

The promises they'd made to always have one another's back.

"Rule number one is no hunter gets left behind," Dallas said seriously.

Malcolm leaned against the hood of

the car while lighting his cigarette, his fresh sun dagger tattoo still stinging his flesh.

Dallas took a swig of his beer as Mal blew smoke rings in the air.

"Rule number two is always finish the job. No matter what," Mal said quietly.

Dallas nodded in agreement.

Mal looked around the quiet, cavernous house that belonged to him now.

Without a body to truly bury, and no family left, the papers were more than clear.

The idyllic 1,800 square foot colonial cottage that once was built for a happily married man and his expectant wife was now just a shell, a dream that would never see fruition.

Home was not a white picket fence for

Jake Dallas or Malcolm Crowley.

Though Mal had spent many nights taking refuge on the road at the house that was now his, it never felt like *home.* Not the way Malcolm remembered it, anyway.

He'd grown up in a house not all that dissimilar to Dallas's on the edge of Salem, oblivious to the truth. He'd even played football and brought his high school team to victory.

But all dreams of happy ever after died for Malcolm when vampires killed his parents and shattered the life they strived so hard to build.

Parents who themselves were *retired* vampire slayers playing house with a white picket fence and two kids who were blissfully ignorant to the true curse of their *given* name.

BLOOD OF THE LOST

Lenora and Peter Crowley had hung up their stakes and traded their name for a shot at the perfect, normal life, and they'd had it for the glimmer of a moment. Fifteen years.

But like everything else, the Crowley curse destroyed them, too.

That was truly the day everything changed, and home became the road.

It became the hunt, the kill.

The endless string of motels and gas stations, and a burning desire in his soul to avenge his parents.

And yet here he was, so many years later, sitting on a soft white couch, alone, mourning the death of yet another person he loved and thought of as family, a person who he knew would one day meet their bitter end at the tip of his blade.

ARIEL DAWN

Because if there was one thing that Malcolm Crowley did better than most, it was kill monsters.

5

DALLAS HAD NEVER been one to stay in one place long, as was the life of a hunter. He'd been living life on the road, between hotel and motel and strange beds in between for so long he could barely remember a time before hunting.

Daylight, it seemed, didn't hold the same pizazz it once had for him now. In fact, he found that during the hours the sun was up, he was much slower, and much more exhausted.

Because you are no longer human.

Although some of that might be because you haven't... fed... in days.

Since that night he'd fed on the poor girl at the Drowned Clam, Dallas kept his distance from most people. When the Djinn went out for their dose of wishes, Dallas stayed in the shadows. He refused to give in to the monster inside of him. Even now, he couldn't stop thinking about the *relief* tasting blood would bring, all the delicacies that lay in it.

And he hated it.

He would have rather kept his distance from the Djinn and the ghouls that followed Amora Medici like a damn circus across Kentucky, but he also wasn't stupid. Monster or not, the small army of minions Amora—better known as *Ami* to the Djinn and ghouls—had formed were not just loyal, but they seemed to be well taken care of, and well... fed.

Despite the fact Midnight continuously told him accepting his fate would ease his turmoil, Dallas could not quite turn off who he was.

A hunter.

He was convinced he just needed something to hunt, some job to distract him from the truth until he'd figured something out. After all, that was what he used to do when things got heavy. Strap on his weapons, load up Mal's car or his bike, and find something to stake.

He knew that keeping close to his enemies, gaining their trust, would be the best option given the circumstances.

Perhaps they would lead him to the answers he sought, some way to cure this Djinn curse he had been infected with, and maybe he could get close enough to the vampire herself, perhaps *she* could tell him the truth about how to cure Ava of her mark. After all, he could be quite convincing, and if not, there was always the end of his stake...

Perhaps, even as a monster, he could do some good.

At least that was the notion he clung to when the hunger pains struck him fiercely, when he found himself questioning himself as he rode on the back of Boo's motorcycle across state lines.

In the week he'd been reluctantly traveling with The Heartsgrave—the official name of the band of monsters who did Amora's bidding—he'd come to learn that plenty of them had skills of their own that went beyond the supernatural.

For instance, Boo, the elder of The Heartsgrave at the tender age of fifty-two—only fifteen years older than Dallas—was fairly skilled at building, fixing, and modding motorcycles. Rebel, though she was a constant thorn in his side with her attitude and snark—qualities he'd found endearing and attractive in Ava, but not so much in the Djinn—was more than just a pretty face. Rebel was smart, cunning even. She seemed to always be a step ahead of everyone else no matter what the situation was, and she was more than formidable when it came to scoping out information ahead of the rest of The

Heartsgrave before they arrived at their location. Not to mention he'd seen her spar with several ghouls from time to time, and judging by the sight of the way she flipped some of them around, she was tougher than she looked.

And Midnight...

The woman he'd intended to question all those nights ago, who he'd charmed into the alley of the Drowned Clam with every intent to do what he was good at—kill his prey—had saved his life, or what was left of it, anyway.

In his guilty chest he could still feel a heartbeat, in his veins he could still feel blood, and warmth.

But his pulse was... slow, steady.

Dallas observed many things about the short, attractive woman who'd 'rescued' him. For starters, Midnight was a watcher, an observer. She kept her eye on everything—the happenings in The Heartsgrave, Dallas's resistance.

The horizon.

She watched the forests they passed, the road they drove, every door that opened and shut.

But what exactly was she watching *for?*

Or rather, *who* was she watching for?

Because if there was one thing Dallas was certain of, it was that Midnight, Rebel, and the others were waiting for some shit to hit the fan. For someone to show up and crash their undead party.

Perhaps they are just waiting for hunters like Mal...

Or worse.

Perhaps they are waiting for Mal...

It was likely they would have seen

him at the labyrinth, and even in the halls where he'd been attacked...

He knew from the newspaper stands, it had been about a week. One single week since he'd been attacked at the Marquis, since he'd seen the proverbial light, and since he'd been brought back from death's door.

He knew without a doubt, Malcolm would have come back for him at some point... despite what Rebel and Midnight seemed to think.

They don't know Mal...

And ultimately, Mal would have put two and two together, once he had come back to the Marquis, and he would make it his job to hunt down the monster Jake Dallas now was.

But the Djinn, the ghouls, and the vampires were enemies to all hunters, and Mal certainly wouldn't have been the only hunter on their tail. Though Dallas refused to feed, a notion which made him feel weak and tired, the Djinn and the ghouls that traveled alongside him did not have such qualms about picking up fast food, leaving a trail in their wake.

If they were smart, they'd ration the bodies, then they wouldn't be so easy to find.

Dallas shook off the thought, despising the road he knew it would lead him down. The innate desire to *protect* his kind was strong, but in Jake Dallas's mind, his kind were on the opposite side of the fence.

Yet despite the trail of bodies in their wake, Ami kept The Heartsgrave moving. They barely stayed more than a night in one place, hopping from motel to motel, city to city in search of some new abandoned, left to rot building to whip up into a honey trap so they could strike again, to pull victims into their web like flies for the feasting. Though Dallas hadn't figured out *why* the Djinn were so loyal to the vampiress, why they continued to work for her.

What was their goal?

Their motivation?

He hadn't figured it out yet. Surely it couldn't have been her hospitality alone, for most off them were skilled enough he was certain they could have made it on their own...

Dallas felt like he was on a bloody merry-go-round he couldn't quite escape.

He didn't want to be one of *them*. But

he couldn't bring himself to kill the Djinn yet. Not when he didn't have enough information on his new... life... or the bigger picture.

Because he was certain as he traveled with the band of monsters that there was a bigger picture.

What other reason would a vampire Queen have to keep moving as she had been?

Most bloodsucking Queens resigned themselves to their thrones, delegating to their soulless lackees and consorts, commanding from behind luxurious palaces and hidden behind warded, hunter-proofed walls.

Yet Amora Medici seemed to be *running*, something Dallas knew very well.

But what exactly was she running

from?

Why did the Djinn run with her?

A knock on his motel door pulled him from his thoughts, and he groaned.

Dallas opened the door to find Boo, the man Midnight had introduced him to at the Drowned Clam, his weathered, tan skin making his trademark Djinn blue eyes stand out against the dusk.

"She's ready," Boo said, with a smile that was somehow both crooked and endearing.

"About damn time," Dallas grumbled as he walked through the door to see the sleek, slender bike in the parking lot.

"Usually I have a bit more downtime, and thus, I probably would have had it done sooner if Ami didn't seem to be in such a hurry," Boo said as he leaned against his blue bronco.

ARIEL DAWN

While the majority of The Heartsgrave rode motorcycles, there were a few individuals, like Boo who drove cars and trucks.

One of the ghouls whose name he hadn't bothered to learn tailed an RV.

Though it seemed Ami herself preferred to travel ahead of The Heartsgrave, and therefore, Dallas hadn't managed to make her bloody acquaintance as a Djinn officially.

Yet.

Dallas walked across the threshold to the parking lot, inspecting the motorcycle. It looked damn near brand new, even though he knew it was nearly fifty years old. Despite the fact Dallas had been brought into the circus that was his life now, Rebel had nonchalantly let it drop they didn't take new recruits often, but that never stopped Boo from loading whatever "diamonds" he came across in junkyards, abandoned on the side of streets, and of course, won during games of pool, in the back of his bronco so he could "tinker" with them.

I bet Tito could own him in a game of pool, though. He'd take Boo for all the bikes he's got.

"It's a start. Once we get'ya a name, I'll paint it on like the rest of 'em." Boo said as he chewed the toothpick in his mouth.

One some level, Dallas wanted to like the man. In a sea of young, pretty Djinn women—the majority of which Ami seemed to favor—Boo stood out like a sore thumb. Djinn men were far and few between. Most of the men in The Heartsgrave were ghouls, and didn't see much light of day, except during travel. The minute they set foot on the pavement of a hotel or motel, they were gone to sleep off the remaining daylight hours until the moon was at its peak.

They were the carvers, the muscle of The Heartsgrave. The "clean up crew."

The ones who... *discarded* the bodies from the labyrinth.

By devouring them, flesh and bone.

Not to mention, there was the fact that Boo was much closer to Dallas's age than anyone else in The Heartsgrave, which made Dallas feel... old.

Thirty-five isn't fucking old, he chastised himself, though he didn't believe it for a second. Despite his appearance, his soul felt just as weathered as the lines around Boo's eyes.

Ami seemed to prefer her honeypots to be young twenty-somethings, which bothered Dallas more than he knew it should have.

The image of Ava accosted his mind, with bright blue Djinn eyes and fangs, and he pushed it out of his mind. Ava may have been thirteen years his junior, and she loved to remind him of that every chance she got. It never bothered him as much as it should have, though. She was sarcastic and guarded, rough around the edges, but soft in the center. She was the one he thought he could never have, and now she would always be the one who got away.

Dallas balled his fist at the thought. He hated how even at this moment, the thought of Ava made him so angry, made him feel so helpless. Though if he hadn't pushed her and her brother out of the way, they would have wound up dead themselves, or worse, a monster like him.

Dallas shook off the thoughts, not wanting to go down that dark road again. The Crowley's plagued his thoughts almost daily, and he knew he needed to put Ava and everything she was as far from his mind as possible if he intended on helping her and her brother from inside the lion's den. If he wanted to keep his mind on the mission.

"Bold of you to assume I'll be here long enough to *get* a name," Dallas said as he ran his fingers over the perfectly shined chrome. As beautiful as Boo's craftsmanship and restoration was, Dallas knew this wasn't *his* bike. His bike, the one he'd built from scratch after he and Laura had moved into their house at the tender age of nineteen and twenty, was no longer *his*.

Because in the event of his death, he'd left everything he had to the only family he truly had left.

Malcolm and Ava.

Not that there was much left to leave, other than a cottage, a bike, and a box of personal belongings that were pretty scarce. Records, high school trophies, photos that would have no meaning left with all the subjects dead or gone.

Though whether or not Malcolm would disclose to Ava that he had indeed left his bike to her, his baby, was another story. He'd mentioned to Malcolm once that Ava loved the bike more than he did, as her eyes always sparkled when she saw it.

After all, it wasn't like he'd told Malcolm he was in fact, in love with his sister.

Though their relationship at best had been complicated, not because she'd been bitten, but because despite his feelings he truly had tried to bury them.

He wasn't abject to having romantic flings or one night stands, and Ava Crowley certainly hadn't been the first young woman he'd been between the sheets with.

Though she was the first since he'd lost the love of his life, that he'd garnered real, honest feelings for.

And now that's fucked.

Still, Boo's gesture, albeit for however long Dallas would be with The Heartsgrave, until he got what he was looking for, what he was hunting, wasn't without appreciation.

Though he knew it probably had more to do with Boo needing to keep himself busy than it did with him wanting to help out a Djinn drifter, a newborn in Ami's band of monsters.

"I call 'em like I see 'em, Dallas. You ain't goin' nowhere 'cuz ya got nowhere else to go." The man's words weren't angry or dismissive, but rather tired and full of empathy.

The need to retaliate and tell Boo where to take his old man musings was strong, but there was a truth to his words Dallas did not want to admit.

Though he could go home—to Albright, Ohio—he knew in the event of his untimely demise Malcolm would have already taken over his home, and would expect him to come back.

And he'd be ready with a knife; ready to stab first and ask no questions. And if he wasn't there, well... Hunter had installed quite the surveillance system, equipped with wards and hexes that would harm and prevent unwanted supernatural visitors. He'd offered to do so the first time Dallas had brought the group back to his house after a brutal mission.

Finish the job, no matter what.

That had always been the number two rule.

No matter what.

And if his home was off limits, certainly Ava's inherited home would be off limits. Not only would Malcolm know in a heartbeat, because Ava would undoubtedly clue her brother in even if he begged her not to, but there was the predicament of the annoying bloodsucker who was never from the blood he'd claimed.

Cassius.

A part of Dallas wondered if his newfound life would make him stronger than a vampire.

Strong enough to rip Cassius's undead heart out of his trim chest and cure Ava of his claim on her blood.

He dismissed the thoughts as Midnight crashed through the clearing, running with haste.

"They're here," she breathed heavily, and Dallas turned his head from the bike in front of him. Boo reached out to steady her shoulders, and it was only then Dallas realized they were shaking.

"Easy there, Midnight, who's where…"

"Vampires," she said as she tried to

catch her breath. "Rebel said she saw them on her scout, she's reporting to Ami as we speak."

Dallas scoffed. "Some run of the mill vamps are the least of your problems, I can assure you. Besides, isn't Ami one of them? What's the big worry?" he said as he started up the bike's ignition.

Boo smoothed his large hands over Midnight's arms, his lips tight.

"Vampire venom is toxic to us. While we may be able to stand our own against them, they are formidable adversaries. And they're assholes."

He looked up from the bike, the purr of the engine below him relaxing his suddenly agitated being.

"You don't say," he drawled.

Midnight's bright blue eyes started back at him with intrigue and mischief.

"You used to hunt them, right? Vampires?" she asked.

Dallas revved his engine a bit before responding. Midnight only had the audacity to stand there with her pale arms crossed, her black tank standing out stark against her fair skin, her breasts shimmering from the sheen of sweat on her skin.

"I *still* hunt monsters, *Midnight.* Wolves, vamps, Djinn..." he said darkly.

Boo grunted in disapproval.

"But you know how to... kill them?"

"Midnight..." Boo cut in cautiously.

Something in Midnight's tone perked up Dallas's inner beast, stirred a hunger that was foreign to his new self, but that which was familiar and desired nonetheless because it was who he'd been since the day he buried his wife.

The desire to hunt, to put a knife through something supernatural was practically making his mouth water.

"Stake, torch, and voila, vamp toast."

"Midnight don't. You don't want to—" Boo's voice edged on caution.

"Why, you want me to go slay you some dragons, Midnight?" he taunted her, his lips pulling back into a sarcastic smile that was somehow also seductive, likely thanks to the Djinn DNA that was slowly working its magic, changing little things here and there about him. His voice, his eyes, his unrelenting hunger.

"I don't want to miss out on the chance—"

Dallas watched intently as Midnight shifted her gaze to Boo, staring at him with longing, desperate eyes.

He could hear the faint whispers, the

wishful thinking of the Djinn in front of him like an underwater echo.

Emma.

One name that held such desire, such hope, and the weight of a thousand wishes reverberated in his brain as he registered that the wishful thoughts were from the Djinn woman who stood before him.

He'd come to understand in the week he'd been traveling with The Heartsgrave that *wishful thinking* was what truly fed a Djinn. Thoughts and desires came to him unabashed when he got near any humans with strong will or emotion, but he hadn't felt such things from a Djinn before. Until this very moment, he didn't even know a Djinn *could* feel the hopes, dreams, and desires of their own kind.

Does that mean I could feed off of her

energy and blood, too?

The idea immediately sent a jolt directly to his groin. He shook off the dark thoughts and the sudden twitch in his cock, feeling a wave of guilt for even thinking such things.

That's like... Djinn cannibalism or something.

But Midnight's wishful thoughts were like a siren's song, and despite the thoughts, he could feel his blood starting to boil, his stomach twisting, and his fangs begging to push through his gums as he set his sights on the fair, raven-haired vixen in front of him.

The faint icy blue haze of her aura was bright to his eyes, and the slow rise and fall of her chest as she met his gaze made his stomach growl and his cock *ache.*

Instinctively, he licked his lips, a stray thought filling his head with wonder as he mused about whether or not a Djinn could bond with someone who hadn't bitten them, what the blood of a Djinn like himself would taste like on his tongue, how their energy would fill him as he filled...

Midnight took a step closer, waving her hand in front of Dallas's vision and immediately all auras and wishful thinking disappeared, as if they were nothing but a figment of his imagination.

He shook his head as he realized she was waiting for him to answer.

Fucking hell D, get yourself together! No fucking bueno! She's a literal monster!

"I, uh..."

"Did you even hear me?" she asked curiously as she stopped just in front of him.

Dallas looked at her, then back at Boo, who had gone stomping off, his arms thrown up in the air as he let out a string of curses.

"No," Dallas admitted honestly.

"I asked if you wanted to go vamp hunting. With me."

"Really? You got an ax to grind with the bats or something?" Dallas raised an eyebrow.

Midnight nodded, her eyes bright and full of aqua glow.

"Or something. What do you say? Are you in or are you out?" she asked, her gaze challenging him.

Dallas got the strangest feeling that he wanted to say 'yes', even though his mind told him it was a terrible idea.

But terrible ideas were a dime a

dozen with Jake Dallas, and the prospect of blood was too hard to ignore.

"I'd say it's about damn fucking time I got to kill something."

6

MIDNIGHT COULD NOT help the hope and desire blossoming in the pit of her stomach.

I didn't think he'd make it this easy...

But before she could lead Dallas across the parking lot, Rebel called out to them. Boo was already halfway across the parking lot by that time, stopping immediately as Rebel waved in alarm.

"Rebel, what's wrong?" Boo asked as

an awful air of tension befell them. Being a Djinn came with many advantages, one of them being an increased sense of sound, sight, and smell.

All the better to understand wishful thinking and our prey...

Rebel looked from Boo to Midnight, who suddenly felt a warmth behind her. She turned her head slightly to see the lumbering former hunter—still present hunter—behind her, his gaze fixated on her.

"Well? Are we going to stand here or are you going to show me a good time?" he said, his voice somehow dark and inviting while menacing at the same time.

Midnight was no fool. She knew that the man she'd saved from undead death would be useful to her, if only because she knew a hunter's skill set could be just as lethal as a monster's. The night she'd met him in the Drunken Clam, she knew then that he was dangerous. She could hear his wishful thinking loud in her head, wishing for the chance to *kill* anything to make him feel better. Hunters had no place in the Clam, especially hunters looking to put an end to her and those she called family now. But something about Dallas then, all tall, brooding and full of deadly instinct was... intriguing to her.

And he isn't all that terrible to look at, either.

But Midnight also knew that a man like Dallas, one who kept to himself, one who put distance between himself and the caravan he traveled with now—including herself—was probably not the most trustworthy person. Especially given the fact she had heard his deathly thoughts before he'd awakened as a Djinn.

I need to kill something. I need answers. This pretty Djinn thinks she's got me, but the only thing she's going to get is my fucking blade.

His thoughts pierced her that night like a veil. She knew she should have walked away, refused his advances. Let someone like Rebel take him on. Just as she knew she should walk away at this moment.

But perhaps, Midnight wanted a little vengeance herself. Leading Dallas into a den of evil vampires could very well backfire, especially if she went in with him alone. He'd made it vehemently clear he had no qualms about hunting

Djinn even now that he was one.

Her memory flashed in her brain, of that first night at the Clam.

Dallas's muscles standing out against the wall as he backed her up against it, boxing her in.

The scent of alcohol, thick on his breath, the fire in his cerulean eyes.

Even as a human, he had rather stunning eyes, the shade something between silvery ghostly apparition and deep ocean blue. She'd never seen anything like it.

Not to mention there was something about his deadly aura that made her feel captivated. His wishful thoughts edged on brutal, but the sadness, the loss beneath the anger and need to kill spoke to her on a level no man alive or dead had ever been capable of doing. Because she understood those things, too.

When she looked in Dallas's bright blue orbs, then and now, she saw a man who was lost.

Her side gaze caught his, and the heat returned to her like it had that night at the Clam when she'd first seen him, that same sense of *desire* blanketing her now as the heat of his breath kissed her exposed skin.

Bad idea, Midnight. Bad fucking idea.

Midnight shook off the momentary lapse in judgment, attributing it to newfound Djinn tactics.

Newborn Djinn often didn't have control of their new skills. They hadn't yet learned how to use their charm to their advantage, and therefore, exuded a sex appeal and aura of desire like a human sweats in the summer. With enough control and mastery, one could use such things to get what they wanted with no resistance. It was how most of the Djinn women in The Heartsgrave operated. A well placed personal or classified ad on the internet here, a meet up on Tinder there, and boom. Luring men and women to Ami's pop up dens of desire and blood was a piece of cake.

They were in the business of granting wishes, after all, and nothing tasted more divine than a lustful, fulfilled wish.

However, the Djinn aura did not usually affect *other* Djinn. Typically, they were immune to one another's auras...

Rebel and Boo looked back at them with worried faces, and it was only then that Midnight realized she'd completely tuned them out, her focus pulled by the hunter behind her who smelled like tobacco and whiskey mixed with cedar and spice.

Who was giving her goosebumps just by standing inches away from her.

Get a hold of yourself, Midnight! You are so much better than this!

Rebel approached her with warning in her bright eyes, her lips pursed into a thin line.

"How much did you hear?" she asked, and up close Midnight could see she was somewhat shaken.

Rebel was like a mountain, there was not much she faltered to.

"I wasn't paying attention," Midnight said, swallowing as she stepped away from Dallas.

"Neither of you heard anything?" Rebel asked as she shot a look at Dallas.

Midnight refused to look at him. His

voice rumbled, stirring up all the debris in her soul when he spoke.

"Don't take it personally, Rebecca. I don't often pay attention to the words of monsters. Usually, I put a blade in them before they can talk."

Rebel pulled her lips back in a sneer, exposing sharp fangs, her eyes glowing with anger.

"It's *Rebel*, you fucking bastard, and while I don't give a shit if you end up monster chow myself, right now we've got a bigger problem."

Midnight reached out, running her fingers down Rebel's arm soothingly. She was rather worked up, and Midnight hated to see her like this. She hated to see anyone upset, naturally. Upset led to anger, and much darker emotions, and even as a Djinn, she could not help but get skittish around such big feelings. It made her feel small, helpless.

"I was reporting to Ami... you know, like I always do... when we were... we were attacked," Rebel said.

Midnight could feel the tremble in her body, in her voice.

"Let me guess, by vampires?" Dallas said apathetically.

Rebel shook her head. "Not just any vampires." She looked at Midnight with sympathy, sighing before she said, "The fucking Boracellis."

Midnight's slow heartbeat stilled to frozen.

Ami had found her entangled in a fight with a vampire from the Boracelli coven. She hadn't known much about vampires or their territories then, being a newborn Djinn herself, thrown into a world of shadow and bone. Nor did she understand how territorial the Boracellis were about who did what on their land. The only instinct Midnight knew at the time was to hunt, to search for what had been taken from her. Feeding on wishful thinking was far and few between for her, for the instinct to consume paled in comparison to the drive of needing to find her daughter, to get her back from the creatures Trevor had given her to.

The Boracellis, it seemed, had been amassing quite the takeover along the east, miles and miles along coast, uprooting nests and covens, and even packs of werewolves along the way, she'd learned once in the care of Ami.

It was the epitome of the wrong place, wrong time for a starving newborn Djinn who'd been hunting for what was taken from her.

Amora Medici saved her life that day. Riddled with vampire venom and temporarily paralyzed, she pulled her from the pavement, skin, bones, and blood. She'd taken her to her rental property, cleaned her up, and offered her what she sorely lacked.

Resources. Food. A warm bed to sleep in.

The Djinn themselves were strong not just in spirit, but in physicality, in ways of the mind, but many of them were alone, wandering the forests and cities with no purpose except to feed. And left to the barest of instincts, these wish-hungry creatures became the stuff of literal legend, a monster to be feared.

Midnight may have been left for dead by her ex and the creatures who took her daughter, but she was not a monster.

She refused to let herself be one, not for herself, but for Emma.

There were not many natural born supernatural enemies that could *kill* a Djinn, after all.

Except vampires, as Midnight had learned that fateful day. The day she was nearly killed by one and saved by another.

***

Amora Medici was a sight to behold on a good day; all fair skin, golden blonde hair, and Aphrodite-like features. She would have made a beautiful looking Djinn, truth be told, but the goddess-like effects of vampirism in her blood didn't hurt her beauty one bit.

Still, it was always somewhat shocking to see the petite woman who looked more like a young pageant Queen than a vicious Queen of blood during their travels.

Ami did not talk about her life, or where she came from often, but Midnight knew she was a Queen among her kind. Queen of the Medici coven, to be exact. Though she hadn't been home to her palace of blood in quite a long time, and Midnight did not ask why. Everyone in The Heartsgrave had secrets, including their leader. It was the thread that tied them all together.

Due to the sudden attack from the Boracellis, Ami had called a meeting in Jackson Hall, an old civil war-era building that looked like it had been stuck in a time capsule. The air was thick with the stench of smoke and old, deteriorating leather, the room bathed in amber light from the dimly lit light bulbs hanging from the rafters.

Not to mention the place was scarcely populated, which made it the perfect hideout for the moment while Ami gathered her band of miscreants for a *kumbaya.*

Dallas, however, seemed disinterested, to say the least. He kept to the edges of the room, near the exit, far enough away that he couldn't be construed as part of the club, but close enough that he could still hear Ami's speech.

To Midnight's knowledge, Dallas and Amora hadn't met officially. After all, Midnight had seen to it that Dallas had what he needed herself—clothing, and the bare necessities, which she'd scrounged from Ami's locker at the Clam herself, and what she could share of her own. It wasn't as if she traveled with much to begin with, her entire life was packed up into a backpack. Though Rebel and Boo pitched in, too, since she'd asked, of course. But Dallas didn't know that. He didn't know the lengths she went to to make sure he was okay, that he was comfortable. After all, she needed him to be comfortable, with The Heartsgrave. With her.

If she was ever going to gain his trust, ask him for his help in finding Emma, she needed him to be.

Though she hadn't planned on introducing him to Ami immediately. And with the fact Ami traveled so far ahead of The Heartsgrave, it was unlikely they'd cross paths unless something like *this* happened.

And Midnight was not expecting an attack from the Boracellis, of all creatures this soon.

Still, she could not help but feel a pang of guilt and jealousy as Amora cast her bright green eyes at Dallas, multiple times throughout her 'give the Boracellis hell' speech.

She had heard it once before, anyway.

Get a hold of yourself, it's not like he belongs to you or anything.

Midnight's lashes fluttered, her lips tightening as the thoughts ran through her.

What Ami did, or who, was none of her business, and despite feeling as if she'd plucked Dallas from death herself, he was a free man. He could do whatever he wanted, and his attitude had made it pretty clear that was how he operated.

So why did the thought of Ami scraping her nails over Dallas's muscles, his sun-kissed skin make her grind her fangs?

Why did the thought of him with a stake held to her own chest make her stomach flip?

"We can always go around them," Boo suggested.

Amora crossed her legs, the motion somehow just as seductive as it was threatening. She focused her eyes on Boo, who was leaning against a brick pillar. In the low amber light, he looked younger than his given age.

While Djinn DNA slowed their heart rates and transformed their features to paler skin, blue eyes, and dark hair, it did not stop their aging process like vampirism did with its victims.

The Djinn were not immortal, despite what the legends said. They aged at a slower rate, but they did age, and their bodies and features reflected it. Boo himself was one of the first members of The Heartsgrave, a former lover of Ami's. He was a handsome man with Djinn attributes, and Midnight wondered for a moment if Dallas would age as gracefully. Standing by the exit, his expression full of boredom, she couldn't deny that he looked positively breathtaking now, but in a few years under the alteration of Djinn DNA, ten or twenty...

"We are not running with our tail between our legs. The Boracellis will be dealt with head on. They think they can strong-arm territories from lesser known covens of this area, covens without the resources to stand up to them. It is lazy, and it is not at all a powerful move. The Boracellis push around those who can not fight. But I will not tiptoe around them. They and their Queen do not frighten me."

"They attacked us—" Rebel spoke up.

Ami shook her head, holding up her hand.

"They attacked us because they thought we were a threat to their stolen territory, which means they are on shaky ground. Shaky ground is what we live for, you all know that. If the ground can be moved, it can be ours. And judging by the newness of the vamp that attacked us, he didn't know *who* he was messing with."

"And just exactly what do you plan to do with this territory?" Dallas piped up, causing Midnight to turn in surprise.

Ami's lips turned up in the corner, a ghost of a smile on her lips.

"And who are you, exactly?" she cooed, just as Midnight opened her mouth.

"He's with me," she said confidently, forcing more than half The Heartsgrave to turn and face her.

"Is that so?" Ami asked.

Dallas grunted. "I'm not—"

"I saved him... at the Marquis. Someone turned him, but whoever it was..."

Ami pursed her lips. "Was likely killed by the hunters who ran us out," she said, her eyes glinting with ferocity.

Midnight nodded in response, feeling a sense of guilt.

Was he with the hunters who had taken the Marquis?

Hunters didn't often travel in packs, but it wouldn't have been completely unheard of that more than one could wind up on the same trail.

Midnight's blood ran cold as she let herself process the thought for the first time. That night at the Clam, she'd danced with the devil, followed him to the alley out of curiosity and a burning desire to consume his deadly wishes.

She'd thought he was the only the hunter in the Clam that night, and though she knew hunters were responsible for the attack on the Marquis, she also knew the vampires Ami had cultivated to be part of her labyrinth would likely draw the attention of slayers. It was inevitable, but she'd never once thought perhaps Dallas had been working *with* them, but even if he had...

Midnight asked herself if she would have saved him if she knew he was responsible for the death of her friend, Enchantress.

She let her gaze settle on him, the fire in her belly returning as she took in the sight of him, all muscles and bright, inviting eyes, a look of apathy on his face that was like a blatant "handle with caution" sign.

And she knew she would have pulled him from the wreckage, even if she'd known there was blood on his hands, blood of those she knew and had grown to care for.

Because regardless of what Dallas had done, she knew everyone deserved a second chance, and fate had given him one, as a Djinn.

Just as it had given her one.

"And you what? Decided to bring someone into my club without my permission?" Ami said, placing a hand on her trim hip.

Midnight realized at once the error of her way. She couldn't tell Ami that she planned to slide Dallas under the radar, keep him as a resource for herself selfishly. For starters, the idea in her head felt more solid than it did at that moment, when she couldn't bring herself to speak the truth, as Amora looked at her with a raised eyebrow.

Shit, I need to figure out a cover, a—

Before Midnight could answer, Dallas

shifted his gaze to her for a moment, his irises glowing like stars in the night sky. He spoke up first.

"I don't ask permission from anyone. I do what I want. And what I want right now, is to stop talking and kill something. Might be you if you don't answer my question."

Chatter sparked among The Heartsgrave as Boo moaned, and Rebel cursed.

Ami only smiled.

"Oh, this little snake has bite," she cooed.

Dallas stared her down.

"Well, my sweet little Viper, to answer your question," Ami said as she rose from her seat, sauntering over to Dallas where he stood.

She stopped in front of him and

Midnight could not take her eyes off him. Off *them.*

"I plan to rebuild, of course. The Boracellis lack the resources to upkeep the territories they steal. I plan to take this territory and give my Heartsgrave a home, a ground to flourish and prosper on, much like I had with the *Marquis* before it was seized from us."

Amora's jade eyes glowed as she bared her fangs at Dallas.

"Before a trusted friend *betrayed* me and sold me out to fucking hunters for human ass."

Dallas stood, still as a statue. Midnight could see the fire in his eyes, the way his jaw tensed from where she sat. The sight was almost imperceptible, but the way he looked at her, the way his muscles tightened... he was holding back.

That she was sure of.

"But you wouldn't know anything about that, would you, little Viper?"

Dallas bore his fiery gaze down at the petite vampiress.

"No, ma'm. I guess I don't," he breathed, his voice dark and full of hatred.

Amora smiled. "I didn't think so," she said as she turned away, leaving Dallas to stand in isolation.

"And what about the vampires?" he asked as Amora gave him her back.

Midnight's blood ran cold.

Amora turned, sweeping her gaze over the club.

"I am not afraid of Eden Boracelli's minions. Perhaps there is room to align them to our side. She's never been the most... liked vampire. Even as a Queen. There are cracks in her foundation, all we need to do is apply pressure. After all, the enemy of my enemy is..."

"My friend," Dallas interrupted.

Amora nodded, twisting her lips. "Indeed," she said as she sat back down, crossing her slender, pale legs once again, her gaze full of ambition and bloodlust.

"Drink up, my dears, we're going to need our strength if we are to reap the treasures we so deserve."

7

DALLAS WAITED WITH bated breath as the woman at the Mayfield Motel ran his credit card again for the third time.

"I'm sorry, sir, it seems the card has been declined."

He sighed in frustration.

"There has to be a mistake."

"I'm sorry, is there another card you'd like me to run?" she asked, and Dallas shook his head.

It had been a week, surely he hadn't run through his limit already... but none of his other cards had worked.

Because you're dead.

The reality hit as he realized in the event of his death, he'd put Malcolm in charge of... well, everything.

He'd left his home, his bike, and his accounts to one sole beneficiary, one he hadn't bothered to change in several years.

Because quite frankly, he had no other family. His parents had passed not long after Laura's death, in an unexpected car accident. With no parents, no wife, no child...

Dallas was well and truly alone. That was, until he'd met Malcolm, Vinny, Tito, and Hunter. *And Ava.*

Surely Mal wouldn't have shut off *all*

of his cards. He would have gone back to discover he had disappeared, and therefore, he'd be looking for him. Tracking his cards would be the easiest thing to do, if he could figure out how to do so. Hunter was usually the tech guy.

Dallas realized as the woman attempted to scan the card once more, perhaps even without Hunter's help, Mal had come to the same conclusion. It made perfect sense.

How could I have been so stupid...

Dallas had been using the card for a week. A motel room here, an order of food there, no issue. But if one had his bank account information, it would be easy to track. And those who had such vital information would see he was making his way west, which meant if the card had been shut off...

Malcolm.

He might be close.

The thought made Dallas panic, and he grabbed the card from the woman.

"It's fine, don't worry about it, I'll figure something out," he said with a smile as she shrugged.

"I'm really sorry," she said as he slid it back into his wallet next to the other two voided cards.

Dallas turned away from the attendant, steadily walking through the lobby toward its exit, needing to get as far away from the place as possible, if only to think clearly. On the way out, he caught his own reflection in the lobby mirror, and it made him stop.

He still looked like himself... for the most part, anyway. He still sported the same tan sheen to his skin, the same thick muscle mass. His dark brown hair was still the same, though it had grown out a bit, and he was in need of a haircut, but his eyes no longer looked... human.

They glowed like bioluminescent algae on the surface of a lake.

Like stars in the night sky.

I'm still me.

His thoughts permeated through the haze of panic that laced through him upon seeing the sight of those monstrous irises that now branded him as something other than human.

Broke, undead, and starving, but I'm still me...

He headed out the door, toward his motorcycle to find Midnight leaning against it, in a pair of tight black jeans, a black tank top, and boots. She wore a large rhinestone crystal cross, which cast little prisms across her smooth skin, her clevage speckled with the fractured light, dark hair falling over her shoulders. Against the backdrop of the rocky terrain, she looked rather... stunning.

Then again, that's how they honey trap you to begin with.

They're made to be stunning and sexy, to lure you so they can feed on your energy, your blood.

Your wishes.

But Dallas shrugged off the notion. All Djinn looked similar, especially the women. Dark hair, pale skin, bright eyes.

Even Boo boasted a bright blue hue to his eyes, and his features were similar, albeit a bit more aged.

Midnight crossed her arms, the motion pushing her breasts together as he slowly sauntered toward her.

"What the fuck are you doing here?" he asked as he gently nudged her away from the seat of his bike. He needed to move, to think.

Riding always cleared his head.

"Got a problem?" she asked as he threw his leg over the seat.

"Nothing that concerns you," he bit.

Midnight settled her hand on his handlebar, covering the ignition.

"Move your hand," he said with a grumble.

"Not until you hear what I have to say," she said.

Dallas sucked in a deep breath.

"I'm not going to ask you twice, Midnight."

"You won't need to, *Viper*," she said with a smirk.

"That's not my name," he nipped.

"Ami gives us our names. It helps, actually. It's easier to leave who we were before the change in the dust. Gives us a new identity, a new life."

"I don't *need* a new life," he said angrily as he grabbed her wrist, twisting it. He hadn't meant to *hurt* her, but it seemed Djinn strength was ten times the among of normal human strength. The bones beneath her skin snapped and popped like a box of rice crispies, but Midnight didn't even blink. It was like she couldn't even feel it...

Before he could even grasp what had happened, she turned her wrist completely around, using the strength to throw him off.

He watched in abject horror as she twisted her wrist around once more, popping it into place.

"What the fuck..." he said in shock.

"You know, I get it. You don't want to accept that this is who you are."

Dallas guffawed, shaking his head. "I don't have fucking time for this bullshit," he nipped.

Midnight did not relent, however.

"I know what you are. A hunter. I knew the moment I saw you in the Clam, when I found you in the Marquis. I know you've done terrible things."

Dallas felt his blood heat, guilt overriding him. Midnight was right, he had done terrible things, to terrible *monsters* who deserved it. Monsters who preyed on humans, hurt them, killed them. Monsters who took without a care in the world as to who or what they'd destroyed.

But something about Midnight's words made him feel... remorseful.

What the fuck?

"And what? You want to try and make me feel better about the fucking *things* I've killed? You think I lose sleep over all the blood I've shed? I don't, and there's nothing you can say or do to change my mind. You think I'm some asshole looking for retribution in your little Amora Medici fan club? I got news for you, Midnight. I'm not sorry for what I've done. I'm only sorry that I didn't stay fucking dead."

Midnight slid her hand over top of his knuckles, and he realized he was gripping his handlebar tight enough he was almost crushing it. Metal bit into his palm, drawing a hint of blood, but it felt *good.* Cathartic even. It reminded him in some weird, twisted way, that he was still alive.

"The universe has given you another chance, Dallas. I know you can't see that yet, but... I've been there, believe me." Midnight implored him with her vibrant gaze, and Dallas fought to get lost in the ocean that she was.

Because when he looked at her, it stirred all the buried, broken, forgotten things inside of him. When he looked at the woman who claimed to have saved him, Dallas's demons rose to the surface. They didn't want to stay buried.

They wanted to be *free.*

But he could not let them out of their cage, no matter how badly he felt compelled to do so, especially to a *monster* like Midnight.

Midnight slowly ran her thumb over his knuckle, the touch feather light. He was surprised to feel it was *warm,* and it soothed his flaring anger, his petrified guilt. So he moved his hand away from beneath her magical touch.

She dropped her hand. "But the sooner you do accept that this is who you are... the sooner you can let go of everything holding you back."

"The only thing holding me back is..."

"Your cards stop working yet?" she asked, and Dallas felt rather on the spot.

"That's none of your business..."

"Mine lasted a few days. Not that I had much in my account anyway."

Dallas started his ignition.

Midnight did not move.

"I was so hungry all the time, so I

spent most of my time hunting down lonely assholes who didn't mind a one night stand. Kept me full and warm for awhile, until..."

"You got a point to this little walk down memory lane?" he bit.

"The Heartsgrave and Ami can help you. I promise."

"Why do you care?" he asked, feeling a sense of guilt and anguish flood his system.

The thought of having to hop from bed to bed, feeding, fucking to stay alive and off the cold, empty streets made him feel like an animal.

I'd rather be put down than have to resort to such depraved things.

Djinn, vampires, even incubi were all nothing more than *parasites* to Dallas. He'd seen them as such for so long, he could barely comprehend the human necessity, the human drive within them.

Because if such things existed within them, then how could they be classified as a monster?

With no money, no answers, and no end in sight, he knew Midnight was right.

Desperate times called for desperate measures.

But was Dallas desperate enough to let a *monster* take care of him?

He knew such alliances, such things would not go unserved. An eye for an eye and all that. If Amora Medici kept him, if Midnight lured him in with her sweet, citrus and woods scent, her endless sapphire eyes... she'd... *they'd* want something in return.

Was he capable of taking the help of

the enemy?

Returning the favor?

Perhaps it would be mutually beneficial...

Midnight threw her leg over the seat, wrapping her arms around Dallas's waist. The sudden movement jarred him, a bolt of electricity sparking through his blood, down his spine as her hands settled on the open skin from his exposed muscle tank. It wasn't the first time he'd felt the spark when she touched him, but he still wasn't sure what to make of it. He hadn't felt such an... energy... when he fed on the mortal woman, and even the graze of touch from Boo or Rebel didn't shock his system quite like Midnight.

Her fingernails traced his skin lightly, making his cock twitch beneath his jeans.

Bad idea, Dallas. She's a fucking monster, and you're...

He couldn't even finish his thought, because instead Midnight spoke.

"Desperate people do desperate things, Dallas. Believe me, I know," Midnight said, her voice trembling only slightly. She tightened her grip on him, her breath on his skin warm and soothing, causing his cock to twitch again.

The deep sorrow lacing her voice spoke to him on a level he could barely understand. Relief, sadness, and longing plagued him as the scent of citrus and vanilla filled his senses. He felt lightheaded as she squeezed him.

"I was lost once, too."

When he did not respond, because for

once in his life, he was utterly speechless, Midnight changed the topic.

"Now, if you're done being a pain in my ass, Ami has asked that you accompany Rebel and I this evening on a mission. We are to head toward the northeast perimeter and gather intel on a property the Boracellis have been guarding."

"Where is your bitchy little bestie at, anyway?" he remarked.

Midnight set her chin on his shoulder, and Dallas could not deny the motion made his stomach flip. It brought back memories of another who used to do the same.

Memories of Laura filled his brain, when she'd curl up behind him in bed, laying her little head on his shoulder, clinging to his much larger body like a monkey, threading her short legs in between his.

Ava didn't like to be spooned at all, nor did she care to be all tangled up in the sheets and held, and she'd certainly never held Dallas after a roll in the hay.

No matter how many times I wanted her to, I never asked. I should have asked.

Dallas pushed the memories away into the dark graveyard of love lost.

"Probably wondering where the hell we are. She left like ten minutes ago."

"What if I said no?" he bit.

Midnight giggled.

"Well then, I guess I would just have to kill some vampires myself with Rebel. Not like I need your help, but I thought you wanted to have a little fun. Wanted to *kill something.* Maybe I was wrong…"

"Next time lead with the killing part, why don't you?" he said as he revved his engine, tearing off into the night with a fire in his blood that fed him in more ways than one.

8

MIDNIGHT WASTED NO time dismounting Dallas's bike. For starters, she knew she needed to be on high alert. Though she'd scouted plenty of places with Rebel before, and she was capable of fending off vampires now that she had a handle on herself, she still felt a sense of fear.

The Boracellis had almost killed her once, after all. But Dallas didn't know that. Not even Rebel or Boo knew that. Everyone in The Heartsgrave had come from circumstances they didn't wish to speak of, and it was a reciprocated understanding that they wouldn't talk or ask questions.

The past was left in the past.

In the days that followed her rebirth under the guise of Ami, she'd found herself regaining confidence and learning how to utilize her skills, thanks to Rebel, Boo, and a ghoul named Harrison who had bit the bullet two towns ago, unfortunately, at the hands of hunters.

Rebel had told her per Ami's instructions, The Heartsgrave would split up into teams and investigate the border of what was believed to be Boracelli territory now, taken over from the Sheehan's. Ami always kept them informed, but only with the information that was absolutely necessary. Though Rebel had disclosed the top secret details, that Ami was not the only one looking to lay down roots.

According to Rebel, the Boracellis had moved their victims—other creatures and children Queen Eden was interested in for her own personal reasons, which couldn't amount to anything good.

Especially considering she kidnaps them.

Rebel was to meet up with Midnight, and *Viper,* as Ami had referred to him, and they were to investigate the east end where the supposed entrance to an old, abandoned estate lay.

An estate that was as monumental as the forest surrounding it, an estate that was secluded and viable to house a group of supernatural prisoners.

I know Emma is in there. If I could just find a way to get away from Dallas and Midnight long enough to see...

Usually, Ami liked to keep herself and The Heartsgrave under the radar, until they'd found somewhere to build, but the estate seemed to be of keen interest to Ami, and therefore, it was an interest to the rest of The Heartsgrave.

After all, the town of Mayfield, Kentucky wasn't as large as some of the other towns or territories they'd traveled through, but if idle supernatural gossip was correct, due to Eden's pressing lunacy, her obsession with finding a way to create the perfect bloodline, the Boracellis had begun to spread themselves thin trying to keep up with the Queen's vamp-napping orders.

Rumor had it that their Queen had yet to produce an heir. Despite having several consorts through the years, most of them meeting their bitter end at her hand. The obsession to fill her womb had driven her to madness, and thus she had given up doing things the old fashioned way, opting instead for a scientific approach.

Blood carries many properties, and blood from fertile creatures like omegas, or from children of powerful bloodlines was what she desired, and she'd worked very hard to steal her resources.

But Midnight wasn't supposed to know any of that. Yet for as much as she trusted the woman who'd saved her life, Midnight knew knowledge was just as powerful as physical strength.

And the more knowledge she had, the better she could use her own skills, her own resources—like Dallas, God willing—to fulfill her greatest wish.

What Ami had told The Heartsgrave, was that the Boracellis needed the territories they stole from other covens, big and small.

They needed to appear strong, because their foundation was crumbling, as Eden sent them all on wild goose chases to find her golden goose eggs, to find her former almost-consort, the one that got away. Castiel or something or other.

And a crumbling foundation meant the entire house would soon come crashing down, bringing an entire empire with it. The Boracellis were one of the last remaining old covens among the vampires, and with any luck Ami would do the noble thing and take it from the psychotic sitting Queen.

A Queen who stole more than territories.

"So what's the plan?" Dallas asked.

Midnight pointed toward the woods.

"Knowing Rebel, she should be on the other side of the forest."

"How do you know that?" Dallas asked, skeptical.

"Can't you feel her presence?" she asked in confusion. Surely Dallas could feel the magnetic pull of the Djinn, being one himself.

It was one of the skills she'd learned early on, when she wasn't certain what had become of her new life as a wish-starved creature. She knew the difference between mortal heartbeats and wishes, and the ebb and flow of the energy of her kind. She also knew Rebel was impatient and likely would have scouted ahead to make sure they had a clear path.

However, in a room full of individuals, a Djinn carried an energy, an aura about them that was like a magnet. Even though she knew Rebel was on the other side of the forest, if she hadn't known, she could still feel her familiar energy, calling out to her own.

"I feel hungry, is what I feel. And annoyed."

Midnight blinked in confusion.

"You don't feel anything?" she asked.

Dallas looked at her for a moment, his gaze surveying her from head to toe. He twisted his lips, as if he was contemplating how to answer, or rather how much to answer. His shoulders tightened and he cracked his neck.

"No. But that doesn't mean I can't track her." He smirked.

"Well, then by all means, Dallas, lead the way if you are so inclined to impress me."

The man scoffed as he headed into the woods.

"Please. I don't need to impress anyone, least of all you."

"That confident in yourself, hmmm?" she taunted him.

"I know my worth. I don't need validation from monsters. Even pretty ones."

Midnight twisted her lips as she followed him into the woods.

"What was that about back there? With Ami?" she asked as she came up beside Dallas. In the thick of night, she could see clearly, thanks to her heightened Djinn sight. Dallas's eyes glowed in the darkness, his face stoic and icy.

"Nothing," he said nonchalantly, but Midnight knew better.

She'd seen the way they looked at one another, and Ami's words had been far more venomous than normal. Dallas was certainly not the first lost boy to join their club of misfits, and Ami had never once been as... cold... when greeting a newcomer, no matter how long they stayed.

No, Midnight knew there was something more underneath Dallas, and she vowed to unearth it. After all, secrets were just as pricey as blood to a vampire, and secrets led to wishes.

Dallas's thoughts were like white noise to her, despite being so close to him. Where they'd been so clear that night in the Clam, and the night she'd brought him back there, where he'd fed on the woman in the parking lot, it seemed his thoughts were hazy at best to her right now.

"Have you hunted her? Before I mean," she asked, trying to keep him talking, and she was curious. She had a deep desire to unearth all of his secrets, though what she'd do with such treasures she wasn't sure yet.

Perhaps she would keep them until she could use them in her favor, though that seemed a little more trouble than it was probably worth, but Midnight had learned in those first few days she'd awakened as a Djinn what she was truly made of.

When push comes to shove, sometimes you discover you've more strength than you realized.

Perhaps if Dallas trusted her enough, she could get him to help her hunt down the vampires who took her daughter. Midnight was not afraid to play a long game, if that was what it took to get Emma back in her arms where she belonged.

"Not specifically her, but..." He stopped, his shoulders tensing as he held his arm out. The sudden motion made him nearly clothesline her, and she opened her mouth to speak, but shut it upon the immediate *look* Dallas gave her. He brought his finger to his lips, his glowing eyes imploring hers with command.

"Don't fucking move," he whispered.

The sudden sound of rustling brush and unmistakable twig snapping was not in the least bit frightening to Midnight, and her instinct was to throw his arm away, to proceed through the forest until they'd reached the clearing where Rebel was...

It's probably just an animal or something.

Except she could no longer feel her friend's aura ebbing beyond the line.

Instead, she could feel it, heavy like a stone, closing in on her, and then the loud, angry roar sounded in the forest, making Midnight's hair stand on end as the scent of *wet dog* assaulted her senses, making her stomach turn.

Rebel's form crashed through the bushes as she grappled with a large, white wolf who slammed her into the ground, teeth bared and snapping at Rebel's neck.

Midnight did not think twice. She only acted on instinct as she threw Dallas's arm away, channeling those innate desires she kept hidden, locked away. Her aura flared in defense, and she could feel the pulsing magic standing on edge as she lunged for the wolf. Her fist made contact with the fur as she screamed, "Hey!" at the lumbering monster.

"Midnight, run!" Rebel yelled as the wolf roared at her with ferocity.

The distraction had worked as he slowly sauntered off of Rebel, his golden eyes fixed on a new target. Rebel lay on the ground, knees to her chest as she tried to catch her breath.

"Go, get out of here!" Rebel hollered.

Midnight continued to stand her ground, her own eyes burning back into the wolf's. Out of her peripheral vision she could see Rebel rise, but she'd lost Dallas. He seemed to have vanished into thin air.

However when the howl sounded, tearing the wolf's attention away, tearing *all* their attentions away, Midnight knew things were only getting started.

The scent of blood, and howls of wolves filled the air, and the faint hint of wishful thinking hit her like a brick.

A deathwish.

The wolf howled in response as it deterred from Midnight's path, taking off in a rush toward the sound of its pack, toward the scent of blood and Dallas once more.

BLOOD OF THE LOST

9

DALLAS HAD ALWAYS been a formidable hunter, if only because he was consumed by vengeance and death. He'd fallen into the world of the supernatural because vampires had killed his wife and unborn child, but even he could not deny that he was... good at it.

Hunting.

Killing.

Saving people from the despair that had happened to him.

He'd pulled people from vampire and Djinn nests, from siren caves, dispelled curses and possessions, and once he'd met Malcolm, his natural bravado, it seemed, had met its match with intelligence and strategy.

Vinny, Tito, and Hunter were all formidable as well, and together they'd been practically unstoppable against whatever foe they faced.

And had he lived past his expiration, perhaps he and Ava could have been a formidable pair as well, given time. She'd shown much promise in that department since he'd trained her himself.

The instinct in Jake Dallas to *protect* was difficult for him to ignore or fight, especially those he felt belonged to him in some shape or fashion.

As a human, he'd been exceptionally perceptive, a trait he'd learned from Mal. It was impossible for Dallas to walk into a room and not know all the exits, to not notice every little sound that could be a potential threat. Yet as a Djinn, he couldn't deny his senses had become extremely heightened.

Midnight seemed surprised he hadn't *felt* the presence of Rebel, as if Djinn could sense their kind like a wolf was supposed to know their pack.

He hadn't the chance to tell her the only thing he could sense was danger beyond the trees. He could sense the vampires, smell the blood and the undulating current of thrall in the air, as well as the wolves beyond the line, and the scent of blood and fur was pungent.

Distracted by the white wolf, Rebel was on her feet as the creature stalked Midnight.

A part of him felt compelled to help her, to *protect* her, but the instinct to do so warred with his own need for vengeance and blood, his own hunger that swelled inside of him like a hurricane.

After all, he'd hunted vampires and monsters for nearly fifteen years. He could not worry about the pretty, sweet-smelling Djinn who made his cock twitch and his blood rush at the moment.

He could not afford a distraction if he wanted to sate the burning desire that was ignited inside of him.

When he'd come to the clearing, the line was clear. Across the way lay an abandoned house, one that didn't look all that dissimilar to the Marquis in size, but by the ornate design, he could tell it was old.

Probably a plantation from the civil war era by the looks of it.

Being a Djinn had come with a multitude of new abilities he hadn't quite mastered or understood yet, but he didn't seem to mind the added visual clarity or the heightened scent. In the night, he could make out the house, the warring wolves, and vampires perfectly.

It didn't matter to Dallas which species of monster met the end of his blade. He wielded it without concern at both creatures, pulling a large brown wolf away from a vampire, a tall, red-headed vampire who reminded him too much of the one he'd found at Terror Con nearly two years ago, though she was not the same one. This one was too tall and much bigger.

The woman snapped her fangs at him, her nails digging into his skin as she tried to fight him off. The wolf lunged for them, its jaw making contact with Dallas's ankle as the vampire shifted them both in its path.

"Fuck!" he growled out as she dug her nails into his flesh deeper, drawing blood as she scraped them down his arm. Heat flushed through his body, his own Djinn aura rising to the surface with pulsating fury. To his surprise, the wolf circled back, but this time it went around him, biting at the vampire's ankles, distracting her enough that she let up on her grip.

Dallas pulled out his blessed knife, his prized slaying weapon, and did not even blink as he shoved it into the vampire's stomach, turning it as his eyes narrowed while he held the tick in place by the neck, his fingers tightening their grasp. He could feel the slow pulse beneath their skin, the unnatural pace. He watched as she gasped, as her body started to shake, as her skin started to turn from fair and smooth to greyed and decayed.

The wolf pounced on the woman in his grasp, shoving her down to the forest floor, large paws on her chest as it threw its head back in a victorious howl. Her decaying body writhed beneath it, giving Dallas just enough time to strike a match and watch the bitch burn.

The sight alone caused a fire in Dallas to catch. Where he'd enjoyed watching vampires go up in flames before, this... this was different.

He could *hear* their dying wish, their pain, and it made him feel good.

The frantic voice of the vampire in his head longed for freedom, for endless blood and love.

The desperation filled him, and it was divine.

Dallas took a step closer, opening his mouth only slightly, sucking in a breath of air, tasting the vampire's wish. The instinct, the *need* to consume its energy that escaped it as it burned in front of him was like drinking a bottle of Jack when he was twenty-one.

It made him feel invincible.

Teamwork makes the dreamwork, after all.

The wolf bounded off the dying vamp, cocking its head to the side as Dallas met its golden gaze.

"Thanks for the assist," he said, catching his own breath. The wolf only huffed, before another howl sounded and it took off.

But victory was short lived as another wolf lunged for him, nearly knocking him over just as another vampire managed to get the one up on him.

Dallas fought their grip as the wolf roared. A quick glance revealed that another vampire had sunk its teeth into the wolf's fur.

How many of them are there?

I thought they were downsizing?

The fuck?

The vampire who held him was male, and he was much stronger than the one he'd just slain. His thoughts were full of one word, one wish.

BLOOD OF THE LOST

Blood.

The overwhelming aura and wishful thinking was combative against Dallas's own desire to prevail and spill this monster's blood. But Dallas was not whole as he once was. He was divided, man and monster trying to co-exist, neither side of him wanting to concede to the other.

And he was burning up.

His entire body felt as if it was aflame, and the instinct inside of him was full of fury and rage. He twisted in its grasp as the vampire wrapped its hands around his neck.

Dallas felt enraged, but he also felt *weak.*

He wasn't as strong as he should have been, because he hadn't fed, something he regretted at the present moment, if only because giving up felt like it would be a blissful release. He could just let go, let the vampire kill him and then he'd truly be gone.

But Midnight's words reverberated in his cerebellum like an annoying echo.

The universe is giving you another chance.

Was the universe really giving him another chance?

To what?

Do things over?

How was that even possible given the state of things?

"It is best if you do not fight me, Djinn," the man growled in his ear.

Dallas twisted in the bloodsucker's grasp, clearly not at will to listen to a monster. As painful as it was, Dallas planted his feet, grabbing onto the vampire's arm with his own strong hands and focused on the one thing he could control, the one thing he knew how to do practically with his eyes closed.

Fight.

Howls echoed as vampires flocked the line, more than he had thought there would be. It was almost like they knew they were coming. Like they'd prepared for this fight ahead of time...

"Fucking let go of me!" Midnight's voice echoed in the air, full of command and anger, and he turned to see a vampire with his fangs inches from her neck, and the world stopped, dimming around him as he was thrown into memory.

The incubus as he sunk his fangs in Ava's neck and she cried out.

Ava twisted and turned in the incubus's grasp, and Dallas was too far away.

But it wasn't him, she cried for as she slumped to the ground when he'd finally made contact with the demon spawn.

No, she did not cry for Dallas.

She cried for Cassius, the vampire who'd marked her.

A fresh flash of fury erupted through him, that burgeoning instinct to protect, to save, overriding everything else. Dallas regained his strength, utilizing it as he broke free, throwing the vampire over his shoulder onto the ground with just enough obliterating force that he'd stunned the creature enough to escape.

In his wake, a wolf closed its maw on the neck of the bloodsucker, the sounds of wet crunching filling the air as Rebel cried out, "Look out!"

Dallas barely had enough attention span to make out her warning, but thanks to his newfound abilities, he *felt* the vampire's movement behind him like a ghost.

He evaded the snapping fangs like the jaws of death, sliding his blade into the belly of the monster, with disregard. He nodded briefly to Rebel, who was clutching her arm, which looked to be covered in blood. She leaned against a tree, heaving with breath as the massacre around them continued.

"Rebel, are you—"

"I'm fine, its not mine," she said as jaws snapped, blood spilled, and it was impossible to differentiate who had done what.

It was truly a bloody free for all.

Though Dallas had only one target, the one in front of him, and he followed Midnight's voice like a ghost, leading him toward some sort of salvation.

Midnight twisted as she grabbed onto the vampire's hands, turning her neck as far as she could from their selfish fangs.

Dallas didn't waste a second as he sunk his blade into the side of the vampire, startling them enough they released Midnight in favor of covering the wound in their side. Dallas removed his blade, covered in black blood, to see the onslaught of liquid seeping out the vampire's side.

"You little parasite..." the vampire man sneered as he lunged for Dallas.

The words were not so dissimilar to what he'd said to many a monster himself, but something about the way the vamp spoke them to him, caused Dallas to black out completely.

He was no parasite.

He was a snake, a viper to be exact.

Dallas's blade fell to the ground as rage filled him, pushing out all thoughts of blood and wishful desires to the edge of his remaining humanity.

For Dallas only saw *red* as he placed his hands around the vampire's throat, watching the sneer, the misguided lust on his face before he snapped the vamp's neck like a damn toothpick, and the rest of the world around him fell to darkness, taking him and his tainted soul with it.

10

MIDNIGHT STARED UP at Dallas from below the fray. The growls and roars from the wolves mingled with the cries and snapping of bones.

But Midnight could not pull her gaze from the tower of fury before her.

It was like he'd become someone else, no... *something* else, something inhuman, something monstrous.

And her heart beat faster at the sight.

His eyes shone bright like neon orbs, his lips pulled back in a vicious snare, fangs fully on display, and the air around her smelled of musky earth, like a storm at sea, all salt and stars and dark forests. It was intoxicating and lit a fire in her that warmed her to her toes.

And when Dallas closed his hands around the vampire's throat, crushing its windpipe with his bare hands, Midnight couldn't help but *salivate.* The vampire dropped to the ground with a slump. Dallas looked almost robotic in his expression, as if he had checked out of himself completely.

"Retreat!" The shrill shriek broke through the din of growls and bites, breaking the spell that had settled on Midnight as she watched the Djinn in front of her. She turned to see the vampires retreating into the shadows, the wolves howling as they pushed them back over the line. A fire still burned behind Dallas, flames from the burning vampire lighting him up like some phoenix.

Or a vicious Viper.

He'd certainly looked the part the moment he snapped and killed a vampire with his bare hands.

Dallas zeroed in his gaze on Midnight. She attempted to move, but she could barely feel her legs, they were numb.

"Fuck..." she growled as Dallas took a step toward her. His eyes still burned like blue fire, and he cocked his head to the side, looking at her like he had that first night in the Clam.

Like she was a monster.

An enemy.

"Viper..." she called, trying to move her legs.

Dallas growled as the wolves that ran around them dispersed, and she had half a mind to try and salvage the investigation, even though she couldn't walk. She'd crawl if she needed to, to find a way inside that house.

She couldn't explain it, but she *knew*.

Every bone in her body knew Emma was there, even though it was probably crazy to assume so. Still, her heart knew her daughter was alive, and her entire being knew she was *here*.

Midnight reached out toward the space, trying with all her might to deadcrawl toward to looming plantation. If Dallas—no, *Viper*—was going to try and stop her, he'd have another thing coming. She'd fight.

She'd always fight for Emma. She'd been doing so for four years.

Dallas did not falter. He was not the same man she'd found on the floor of the Marquis. Amora had been right to name him as she had. Panic and desire flooded Midnight, warring together within her soul. Wishful thinking threatened to blossom out of her psyche, and she could feel *him,* his Djinn aura pulsing in the air, his scent filling her airways, like a sedative drug. Coaxing her and her wishful thinking into its web. But she was afraid of giving up the one thing that could truly kill her without a sound. She could use the help of someone like Dallas, sure. But giving him access to her heart's biggest wish would be tantamount to giving him the power to utterly destroy her completely.

For if a Djinn said those two fabled words, "I wish", to another Djinn...

It was giving them the power to grant it.

It was rare a Djinn granted the wish of another Djinn, and feeding on their own kind was practically forbidden. A Djinn who fed on its own kind, if strong enough to hold that much energy, would have the power to grant *living hearts* wishes, not just those made in death. A Djinn that powerful was capable of unspeakable things.

"Don't let them get away..." she cried as she attempted to stand, pushing herself up to only stumble like a newborn fawn. Her gaze caught the eyes of a white wolf, its amber irises rimmed in gold as its pack moved alongside, in the opposite direction. The vampires were not the only ones to retreat. Its golden orbs stared back at her, cocking its white head to the side as it took a step closer. She could feel her wishful thinking solidifying, begging to latch on to something, anything that could save her from a familiar fate, give her the strength she needed to rise and take back what belonged to her.

Midnight lay on the ground of the forest in the woods, her body immobile. She'd lost so much blood in the attack.

Her lungs labored to breathe, but it hurt. Her ribs had been shattered, and blood seeped out of her chest, and her body was cold, so very cold. She tried to speak, but there was only blood. She watched as her ex handed Emma off to a tall, raven-haired creature.

They'd been ambushed, or so she

thought.

She'd fought one of the creatures off at first, but Trevor stopped her with a hand around the throat, and fire in his eyes.

"Don't move," he said with a snarl, twisting her neck as he shoved it back in the ground.

"What do you wish for?" the creature asked as she flashed her bright blue eyes at him.

"Freedom," he said as he handed their daughter over to the creature.

The woman reached her fingers out to touch Trevor's cheek, opening her mouth to reveal stark white fangs as the color drained from his face.

Emma clutched the stranger's shoulder, her head turned away from the supernatural sight.

Midnight cried out for Emma, for

Trevor to reconsider, to get up and fight, but there was no sound except the gargle of the blood in her throat.

Because I'm dying, she realized.

"I said, don't fucking move," Dallas growled as he stopped before her, looking down at her on the ground.

"No, please..." she begged, wondering if this was it. Memory danced with the present, blinding her as exhaustion slid up her body like a snake.

If this was truly it, then fate had dealt its final hand in punishment for what she'd done, what she wasn't capable of doing, and all that she had lost.

She'd thought if she gave the *Viper* in front of her the resources she never had when she'd awakened as a Djinn, perhaps she could do something right. But perhaps that was Midnight's flaw, both in human existence and in this deadly one. She was too trusting, too much of a dreamer. She only ever saw the good in people. Even when they were classified as monsters.

She'd dared to hope, despite having everything taken from her. Hope that perhaps this death sentence could be worth something more than just consuming the dying wishes of mortals, that somehow she could save others, the way Ami had saved her when she'd found her struggling with the onslaught of a new life.

The blinding sight, the loud surroundings, and the pain and blood... the hunger...

She would never get that chance now, to turn this curse into a blessing, she thought as she closed her eyes. But the hands of death around her throat never came. Instead, she felt large, strong arms lift her from the ground, heard Rebel's heavy breathing beside her.

"Is she..." Rebel's voice shook.

"She's breathing, isn't she?" Dallas said darkly.

She felt the air around her, crisp like a ghostly blanket as the sound of trampled leaves and howls reverberated through the air. Her mind danced with the image of Trevor, and Emma's small fist as it curled in the raven locks of the creature who'd taken her. Memories of Emma's sweet laugh only earlier that day as she blew bubbles on the cabin porch, slopping bubble solution everywhere, meshed with the memory of Trevor attacking her, telling her to 'stay down and just die', juxtaposed with the sound of Dallas's heavy breath.

Dallas...

"Dallas..." Midnight's voice came out an exhausted whisper as his scent hit her. Up close, against his warm, solid chest, it was impossible to ignore, and she couldn't help as her entire body relaxed in his hold. "I need to..." she choked out, the words like feathers in the air.

The instinct to burrow against him, to slide her arms around his neck, was more than overpowering. His energy, his aura was all enveloping as he tightened his grip underneath her legs, which still felt numb. But such things went against *everything* Midnight knew.

Past mixed with present as it all converged on her at once. She needed to move, she needed to get to Emma, to save her, to...

"They're getting away..." She moaned, feeling the beginnings of slumber begging to pull her under.

"It's okay, Midnight, you're going to be okay..." Rebel's voice cut in through the echo of pain, the haunting memory.

The darkness pulled Midnight under, and she was powerless to stop it. She let it consume her, as the creature walked off with her child, leaving her and Trevor to die.

How could she make him understand?

Speaking was difficult.

Midnight slid her hand across Dallas's chest, feeling the solid carved muscle, warm and smooth. His heartbeat thundered against her palm, her consciousness fading due to the vampire's venom in her system.

I wish you could understand... she thought the words, and immediately felt a jolt of electricity, leaving her fingertips like magic, seeping into Dallas through his sweaty shirt, into his defined chest.

His grip tightened on her, and she could feel his heartbeat quicken, the small gasp from his lips almost unnoticeable as she closed her eyes and let the memory run its course.

She let her mind wander through the labyrinth of her internal shadows, trying to piece every fractured moment together with stitching she didn't have.

Memories of wolves and vampires fighting in the wood, of a lumbering hunter with deadly blue eyes, of a beautiful creature who looked her square in the eye as she took everything that belonged to her.

She'd never quite seen another creature take down the vampires as efficiently as the wolves had, when they'd corralled the creatures, working in their pack to take out the threat. It was like they were *helping* them.

But that would be crazy, right?

Wolves were known to be isolated, and loyal to their packs. They rarely got involved in supernatural squabbles. They kept to themselves, out of everyone's hair. But it was clear they had skills. Skills that could be helpful to a band of Djinn, if she could just *heal* fast enough...

Dallas and Rebel were not without their own skill set either, and together they had killed several vampires in the attack as well. Somehow Midnight knew they needed the wolves.

There was a strong probability that perhaps the wolves knew more than they did. After all, they were there, warring with the vampires when she and Dallas had arrived. Perhaps there was a reason the wolves were attacking on the very same land.

Instinct told Midnight Emma was in that house, but she knew the Boracellis were kidnapping more than just children... she'd heard the whispers of *omegas* in passing when Ami didn't think she was near. Perhaps the Djinn were not the only ones fixing to put an end to the Boracelli bastards, which meant they could be allies.

I have to tell Ami, I have to—

A voice cut through her psyche, rough and jarring.

You need to give it a rest and get out of my fucking head!

Midnight gasped audibly, writhing a bit in Dallas's arms.

I don't know how, she thought. *I don't...*

Dallas spoke aloud, his voice a dark whisper.

"Just let go, Midnight. Stop fighting. I've got you, you're safe."

The sincerity in his whisper, the pain laced in those words... It was as if he'd said them before.

Midnight couldn't explain it, but the words were like some sort of innate command she was powerless to resist. In fact, she could not answer, only fall victim to the darkness that called her. Crushed against Dallas's warm chest, his heart thudding away like a lullaby against her ear, she had no choice but to give in.

Emma's green eyes looked at her as she yawned.

The woman carried her away.

Trevor fell to the ground with a thud.

A tear streamed down Midnight's face, and she wished for the moment that when she woke, the nightmare would be over, and Emma would be back where she belonged.

11

DALLAS SAT ON the edge of Midnight's bed, with his head in his hands.

She slept soundly, soft snores escaping her chest as if she hadn't been a part of a melee in the woods.

Dallas knew more than most from years of hunting monsters. Lore was rampant if you knew where to look. But ever since he'd awakened as a Djinn himself, it seemed in actuality, he knew *nothing.*

Djinn weren't supposed to be able to have telepathy with one another, that he knew for sure, and Boo had confirmed the suspicion when he'd arrived with a sleeping, limp Midnight in his arms on the motel property.

Boo had seen them and immediately brought them to his room, where they'd been since. Dallas, and Rebel had been quick to brief him while Rebel set about to cleaning herself up.

Dallas had refused any treatment. He hadn't sustained any injuries except for his wolf bite, which was already healing and less itchy. He'd been bitten by animals before, albeit those animals were not supernatural shifters, but Dallas could not focus on himself.

Every particle of his being felt an

astronomical pull to the woman who lay on Boo's bed, her dark hair splayed around the white pillowcases, her pale pink lips parted just enough to let out those tiny, soft snores that were somehow adorable, despite the given circumstances.

In the light of Boo's room, she looked innocent. Like some sort of raven-haired angel, all dark eyelashes and pale skin, her glittering cross stuck between her cleavage as she slept on her side.

Dallas carefully moved the chain, laying it on top of her chest instead. Her skin was cool to the touch, a welcome relief from the heat of his own body. He was sweating, his adrenaline through the roof.

You did just kill some vampires, and found out you can mindspeak with another monster. That's enough to rattle anyone...

Rebel stood against the wall, her arms crossed, her blue highlights shimmering in the low light.

Boo let out a deep sigh.

"It was a trap," Dallas said as he ran his hand over his face. He had come to the conclusion somewhere between the walk to the bikes and their arrival at the motel. He clutched Midnight to his chest the whole ride back, some twisted sense of feeling like a hero racking him as they got further and further away from the estate in the woods.

The more distance he traveled in the night with her body pressed against him, the clearer the truth became.

The truth about the Boracellis, anyway.

"If you would have shown up on time..." Rebel bit, but Boo only held his hand up.

"No, he's right. It was a trap. You were not the first team to make it back with an injured victim. The Boracellis are sending a message. To Ami."

"Who else..." Rebel's eyebrows furrowed, her jaw tightening.

"Gorgon, Strega, and Chewy all came back with injuries."

"Are they... severe?" Rebel asked warily.

Boo sat down in the rickety chair at the makeshift table by the door.

"Gorgon and Chewy seem to be all right, minimal venom, like Midnight. Strega got the worst of it, she's..." Boo's voice faltered, and Rebel slowly walked over to him, sliding her hand up and down his back in a way that felt almost as if Dallas was witnessing something intimate, private.

"And we should be concerned because..." Dallas raised an eyebrow.

Rebel shot him a glare. "What does a vamp bite do to a human, without feeding?"

Dallas leaned his arms over his knees, before meeting her gaze.

"A bite without feeding can turn a human to a vampire, if the vamp's got the juice, that is. Everyone knows that."

Boo ran a hand over his face, a deep sigh leaving him. "Multiple vampires bit Strega. It'll be a miracle if she regains her mobility," he said softly.

Rebel nodded. "Vampire venom is toxic to us. It can paralyze us if it doesn't fucking kill us."

Dallas sat up straighter at her words. He'd been versed enough in Djinn lore from his last hunt with Malcolm, the very one that led him to the Marquis. Hunter had told him the Djinn were powerful, that they needed hopes and dreams, and innermost desires to sustain themselves, but they weren't difficult to kill if you could get past their witchy-woo mind tricks, which were a thousand times more intense than a vampire's thrall. They weren't immortal, after all. A regular blessed blade would do the trick.

However, their charms were something off a hallucinogenic when feeding on wishes and desires. A Djinn could craft your wildest dreams, present them before you in an illusion so real, you'd beg for it. But not once in Hunter's research had they come across information like what Rebel was presenting. It seemed like a trade secret the monsters most certainly wouldn't want in the hands of hunters.

Vampire venom was toxic to Djinn.

Midnight had mentioned the venom was toxic, but he'd dismissed her words if only because they'd been interrupted before she could explain how or what it did.

It was true that most supernatural creatures were territorial, and most liked to keep to their own monstrous communities and units. Supernaturals did not often mingle with one another, but to learn that a creature like the Djinn could be taken out with something as simple as vampire venom was both a startling piece of information and a helpful one.

A knock on the door made Dallas and Rebel nearly jump out of their skin.

After everything that had transpired, he wasn't sure he trusted himself, let alone any of the monsters in the same room with him.

The memory of snapping the vampire's neck, of the scent of its decay, made him hungry even now for more bloody deathwishes, and he hated it.

He hated that he *needed* to maim and kill to feel sane. He hadn't needed to do so when he was... alive.

Well, maybe that's not entirely true.

But he knew he wasn't really dead either, and the woman in the bed only a few feet away from him wasn't dead either, despite the venom in her blood, and for that Dallas felt rather relieved, which didn't make a lick of sense to him.

He looked at Midnight as a sense overcame him to *protect* her. Like a cat whose haunches rose when they felt threatened, Dallas instinctively rose and moved in front of Midnight, blocking whatever monster lurked beyond the door from her.

Why do I care whether she lives or dies? She isn't anything to me...

He thought the strange thoughts, but even as they sounded in his head, he knew they were not true.

She'd managed to touch him, to link with him and his thoughts.

And he couldn't deny that when she set her palm on his chest, it *soothed* all the turmoil roiling inside of him at the moment. It was like magic, like she was the peace and bliss he'd been searching for since he lost his wife.

But that didn't make any sense either, and so Dallas did what he did best when things were too difficult to think about. He buried them deep down.

He wasn't entirely sure who or what Midnight was to him. Once, she'd been his mark. He'd picked her out of the crowd because she was a Djinn, because he thought she'd be easy enough to charm into giving up the information they needed to get into the Marquis at the time. He'd picked her because she was attractive and he could have bet that she'd fall into his devil may care dominant attitude, like most women did. He hadn't chosen her out of the Clam's crowd because he felt some sense of undeniable attraction to her, after all she was the enemy. She was a *monster*.

But now Dallas was not so sure.

She was a monster, yes, but she was also a woman. A woman who had saved him, when he'd awakened, cursed.

She claimed that she 'saved' him, but had she really?

What reason did she have to do so?

In Dallas's life, he had learned that there was always an endgame, after all. He wasn't certain what hers was, but he would get to the bottom of it one way or another.

What would have happened if he hadn't run off with the Djinn?

Would Mal have found him?

The cops, even?

Would he be halfway to getting this Djinn curse off of him, somehow?

Would they have already found a cure?

Or would he have wound up fangs deep in a blood massacre trying to feed the monster inside of him until Mal or a hunter put him six feet under?

Would he be back in Chester with Ava and her mood swings, wondering if she loved him?

Dallas pushed the thoughts aside as Boo opened the door. Now was not the time for a walk down anxiety lane. There were bigger problems he needed to deal with.

Like the vampires who could probably kill me, and the Djinn who can read my fucking mind.

Amora stood in the doorway, dressed in a pink sweater with white stars, and light blue jeans, her golden hair curled perfectly at the tips. For a vampire, she looked rather young, though such an assumption was moot when it came to the creatures of the night. Vampires tended to stay in the appearance of the age they'd been turned, and judging by Amora's appearance, Dallas would have surmised she was not a day over seventeen or eighteen. Though he had no idea how old she truly was, nor did he care. Age was nothing but a number, especially when it came to the supernatural.

But he did know that she was likely old enough to be friends with Cassius, the vampire who'd marked Ava. He'd seen the glimpse of them in the Clam, and even in the Marquis. Though Cassius was remiss to tell them anything that could have truly helped the situation at the time, in favor of chasing Ava, despite the fact Dallas knew he'd never have her.

Ava was smarter than that, not to mention they'd been training for the very moment she would drive a stake through his chest for *years*.

Despite Cassius being as unhelpful as he was, it was apparent however, that Amora was more than powerful enough to have amassed a labyrinthian masquerade in the middle of nowhere where wealthy vampires bought spots for their own mortal hunger games, just for blood sport. Which meant she had connections, and a reputation, which meant she had access to more than she let on. And if Dallas played his cards right, slid into her good graces, gained her trust... perhaps that could be most helpful for him.

In the light of Boo's motel room,

Amora suddenly didn't look menacing at all.

In fact, she looked like an innocent teenager from a nineties sitcom.

"What do you want?" he asked, his voice coming out much more bitter than he'd intended.

"I am calling an emergency meeting. This attack on my clan, on my Heartsgrave, I will not stand for it. The Boracellis are getting too bold, and frankly, someone needs to put them in their place. I will need all of those who are able to meet with me in Jackson Hall to do so in ten minutes," she said plainly.

The sight of her nonchalance annoyed and angered Dallas.

How could she stand there like that, when it was her *clan* that had taken a beating for her at her command, already?

Because they don't matter to her. They are expendable, and you are no different. You need to remember that. You need to get as far from these monsters as possible.

"I didn't sign up for this," he said, shaking his head.

"That may be true, but I have been told you were quite... helpful, on your investigation."

"Is that so?" he asked skeptically, glaring at Rebel. She had arrived nearly ten minutes later to Boo's motel room after they'd arrived, no doubt reporting to Chief PinkSweater.

"I believe we could be of assistance to one another, *Viper*," Amora said sweetly, her green eyes sparkling like deep emeralds against the low light of Boo's motel room.

Dallas's jaw tensed. He did not like Amora's insinuations, but something told him she was right.

Midnight, Rebel, Boo, and the rest of The Heartsgrave were all well kept by Amora, that was apparent in how they traveled. As long as he stayed with The Heartsgrave, he was likely to have at least the bare necessities, funds or no funds.

"And what about Midnight?" Dallas asked, his lips pulling back into a snarl. "The injured just get left behind like the trash you think they are?" he asked.

Ami's lips twisted up in the corners as she crossed her arms.

"The *injured* as you say, will require a caretaker while they heal, and therefore are not required to attend this emergency meeting."

"Venom is a bitch," Rebel started as she stepped forward. "I will stay with her," Rebel said, causing them all to turn in unison.

"No, I'll stay... you should go, you are one of our best scouts," Boo offered.

"Viper will stay. It is clear *he* needs to learn many things about how we operate," Amora said, her tone full of command.

"He has no idea how to treat venom sickness!" Rebel hollered as Dallas bit, "That's not my fucking name!"

Amora did not flinch. She only looked bored with the conversation.

"I think he can handle babysitting a sleeping Djinn for a night, Rebel. Unless you don't trust *my* judgment."

Dallas wanted to object, but Rebel shook her head slightly.

"Of course not, Ami," Rebel said, dropping her tone to a much more submissive one.

Don't challenge Buffy the vampire. That means she is afraid of her, which means she doesn't trust her. I can work with that.

"Good girl. Now that's settled. Viper, you will stay with Midnight. If she awakens during that time, make sure she eats and keeps her strength up, and don't let her do anything too strenuous. I'm sure you can handle that," she said, her voice drenched in thick a practiced sweetness. Sweetness that hid the command, the bitterness in her eyes.

"Fine by me," he said darkly.

Boo's eyebrows furrowed as he looked

at Dallas with concern, but it was short lived.

"Come, we have much to discuss," Ami said as she disappeared from the doorway into the night once more, Rebel and Boo following in her wake.

In the silence that followed, Dallas felt like he could finally breathe, and so he let out a deep breath.

"What the fuck am I doing?" he asked out loud, musing to himself.

With Amora and the judging looks from Boo and Rebel finally gone, he let his shoulders fall in defeat.

"I didn't fucking ask to be dropped in the center of some supernatural war or some shit, fuck," he said as he leaned back on the bed, his fingers gripping the comforter.

"Not to mention, there's the whole

you're running out of money problem, the fucking mindspeak thing..." He sighed, staring at the ceiling.

All the problems seemed to be catching up to him, and he was no closer to solving them than he was when he'd woken up on the floor of the Marquis a week ago.

"You need to find a way out of this... You need..."

"You need to be quiet. How's a girl supposed to get any sleep around here?" A groggy voice pulled him from his thoughts and he turned quickly to see Midnight pushing herself up. She looked pale, paler than a Djinn probably should.

But she was alive.

"You're..."

"Haven't been knocked on my ass

that good in a while, that's for sure," she said as she slowly moved her legs. The breath she let out was full of relief.

"Oh, thank the lord I can move them... better than I could before..." She huffed out as she fell back against the headboard.

"Damn vampire venom," she grumbled. "Stuff stuns the hell out of you if you're not careful."

"It can kill you, too, right?" He asked.

Midnight shook her head. "Yeah, it can kill us. If you've got enough of it in your blood, that is. But it would take a lot of vamp venom to do that, like multiple bites from multiple vamps. But that doesn't mean a single bite of venom can't paralyze us."

"Stop saying 'us.' You keep saying us, like I'm one of you," he grumbled.

He wasn't sure why he felt so agitated. Though he couldn't deny that one word, 'us' made his heart beat a little faster.

It's just all the adrenaline, it has nothing to do with the pretty Djinn on the bed next to you...

Midnight's eyes softened. "Because you are one of us, *Viper*. Even if you don't see it, yet," she said, her voice like a whisper on the wind.

"That's not my name," he said evenly. Midnight's lips twisted in a sweet smile. Her expression was endearing, sweet even. Her blue eyes sparkled in the light with a little mischief.

"I know, Dallas," she said.

He wasn't sure why he felt such an overwhelming need to tell her his name, his real name, but he did. And the compulsion was too difficult to ignore, despite its implications of what doing so meant.

"My name is Jake. Dallas is my last name."

Midnight scooted a little closer and he pretended no to notice.

Dallas shoved the strange feelings down into the dark coffin of his soul with the rest of the things he wanted to bury.

I am nothing like these monsters.

I am a hunter...

Amora had dispatched her team to *hunt* the vampires, but it wasn't just vampires they'd found.

"They knew we were coming," he said, if only because he needed to change the subject and bring her up to speed. He looked away from Midnight, hoping that his racing heart would even out again, but it didn't.

The air between him and the raven-haired vixen was thick and heavy, like his breathing that would not return to normal.

"There's no way. Rebel had only just gotten the location before I came to find you…"

"Maybe someone else in The Heartsgrave has already switched sides. Think about it."

"No one in The Heartsgrave would dare to defect to the *Boracellis*," Midnight snapped.

Dallas turned to face her, noticing the fury in her eyes, the anger in her voice.

The disdain for the vampires was more than prominent, which told him Midnight saw them as foe and not friend, as Amora did.

Definitely not Midnight, then. Though that anger comes from somewhere. I'd bet she has some kind of history with them.

"Boo said others were harmed on their scouting. They were prepared for us, which means they knew we were coming. There is definitely a snake in the well. Someone gave us up. Which means The Heartsgrave isn't as loyal as they appear."

"Really? You embracing all the snake references now just because Ami gave you a name?"

"I wasn't—"

"Relax, *Jake.* I'm just pulling your chain. Though, I have to admit, back there, you did kind of look like one. A viper, I mean. You struck like one, too. Name more than fits," she said calmly.

The way she said his name, his real

name... was like the contented purr of a cat, or a kitten.

Dallas dipped his gaze to the cat tattoo on his forearm, the one that was still fresh. He'd only gotten it a month ago, on a whim. He knew better than to tattoo a woman's name on his body, but no one would ever know he called Ava 'kitten', and therefore they'd have no idea he'd gotten it for her. Not even Ava herself suspected anything.

But as he looked at it, rubbing his thumb over the crescent moon in the middle of the cat's head, he had to admit he didn't feel the remorse he expected to.

He only felt lost.

Midnight pulled herself closer to Dallas, and he pretended not to notice, even though the sugary sweet scent of vanilla cake batter and citrus filled his lungs with relief and desire.

Midnight leaned forward, inching closer to him, her scent thick like a fog around him. Her aura ebbed, its gravitational pull difficult to ignore.

His thoughts threatened to go awry, and he had to fight the urge to let them run away.

"Jake," she purred once more, her voice seductive and warm, inviting. It was as if she was really tasting it for the first time, recognizing the gift he'd felt *compelled* to give her. His name on her tongue was like black velvet, the fabric and the liquor.

Smooth, addicting.

"Midnight..." he cautiously spoke, his own voice edged with a darkness that he couldn't control. He breathed her name like a warning. But she did not fear him as she should have, and Dallas wasn't sure how he felt about that.

His gaze flecked to hers before dipping to her lips as he shifted his weight on the bed, both wanting to get as far away from the pretty Djinn as possible and to shift the sudden erection he'd sprung from the purr of her voice. Not to mention the overwhelming desire of wanting to feel her skin against his again as he had when he carried her home.

Home.

The Mayfield Motel was not *home.*

Home was in Albright Ohio, in the back of Malcolm Crowley's candy apple red Chevelle.

Home was not the middle of Kentucky with a motorcycle club full of monsters.

Or a one motel room with a beautiful

woman whose voice made his cock twitch and who could read his mind.

I hope she can't hear me right now...

Dallas got up, needing to put some distance between himself and the bed.

He slowly sauntered over to the window, peeking through the blinds. The silence in his brain meant perhaps she couldn't hear his thoughts, or she just didn't care to push him.

"How'd you get yours?" he asked, changing the subject. "Your name, I mean? Surely you weren't born with the name Midnight." He needed to change the topic, if only to keep her talking, to keep his mind from focusing on all the things he knew he shouldn't. Like the sight of her bountiful, milky white breasts sleek with a sheen of sweat, spilling out of her top, or her perfect, pouty lips that he thought would look beautiful wrapped around his aching cock. Her cross that glinted in the low room's light, which had fallen into her cleavage again.

Dallas grunted, shoving the thought aside.

He could see the reflection of her in the motel room mirror, of her bright eyes and long hair that fell over the swell of her cleavage in her tank top, the slender curve from her back to her ass from the angle of the reflection.

"Clock struck twelve when she found me. I was pretty much struggling when I came to."

"Sounds like you should be Cinderella then, instead."

"Well, the slave part would fit, but I'm not so sure about the princess part. My prince charming might have had the charming part down, but he lied about the rest of it..."

"So Midnight struck, and he turned into a pumpkin?"

"Something like that."

"Sounds like a catch," Dallas said.

"Yeah well, when you're young you think everything will last forever, you know?" she said, her voice full of sadness and remorse.

"Pffft. What are you, like twenty-three?"

"Twenty-nine, actually," Midnight said with a slight smirk. "Retrospect is always clearer, you know? Like, the things I wish I knew when I was twenty-three..."

The sound of her wistful voice made him turn around to see her trying to get up off the bed, her knees buckling. In a flash he was by her side, almost instantly as he caught her just before she fell.

"Unfortunately, I do know," he said as he caught her in his arms, the little shockwaves from her touch coursing through him like lightning.

"Christ, you're fast. Faster than most of us when we're newborn."

Her fingers sprawled out on his skin, nails grazing along his muscles.

He steadied her with his hands around her waist, and she clutched his arms for support. The motion put her against his chest, against his hardening cock.

Now is not the time, for fuck's sake!

Midnight looked up at him with glassy, supernatural eyes, searching his for something he wasn't quite sure of. Some raven hair fell over her shoulder, the edges tickling his knuckles.

He'd always loved a woman with long hair. Laura always tried to grow it past her shoulders, to no avail, and he couldn't deny he'd loved grabbing Ava by the ponytail when she had long hair. She'd cut it shortly after they'd started training, after he'd grabbed her by the ponytail and whipped her around like a damn rag doll, and though he'd grabbed it more than once on occasion after she'd cut it, twisting his fingers in the locks, it didn't have the same feel, the same tension that he favored.

His body flared with heat from the touch, and when her gaze fell to his lips, when she didn't make a move, he couldn't help himself. The desire, the urge was too overpowering.

Instinctively, he couldn't help himself as he looked back at Midnight and her vibrant eyes, and impulsively he ran his thick fingers through her hair, if only to brush it back over her shoulder. It was soft, smooth, and he wanted to repeatedly run his fingers through it, the motion soothing and comforting to his own internal turmoil. It was a swift, impulsive movement as he brought his lips to hers, savoring the sweet vanilla taste of her lips against his own.

Midnight's breath hitched, and her breasts heaved against his chest from the motion, the surprise there evident. Though she recovered from her awe quickly, relaxing in his hold, melting in his arms, returning his sudden kiss.

She tasted like *home*. Like every wish,

every dream he'd ever had rolled up into silky smooth, sweet lips. She tasted like *magic*. And when she parted her lips just enough for him to really taste her, with his tongue, Dallas knew nothing would ever be the same again.

Because Midnight tasted better than blood, better than wishful thinking, and he wanted more.

She trembled in his grasp as she pulled away slowly.

"How are you doing that?" she asked, her breath, half a whisper.

"Doing what?" Dallas asked, his voice somehow darker than he'd intended.

"Your scent...your energy is like... it's like it's... feeding me..."

"You can smell me?" he said as he wrinkled his nose, backing away with sudden concern.

Midnight giggled, and the sound was almost angelic. Almost

She didn't move from where he held her, and he didn't push her away. Instead, they stood there against the bed, Midnight leaning into him comfortably. The feeling was... nice and fed him in more ways that wishful thinking had. She fit in his large arms quite nicely.

Perfectly, like she was made to be here.

The thoughts cut through him, causing his cock to twitch once more, his body warm from his head to his toes.

"All Djinn usually have the same scent. Spicy citrus, musk. Vanilla, sometimes. But you... you smell different. It's a good different, though. I... like it."

"What do I smell like?" he asked gruffly as his gaze dipped to her lips. The overwhelming desire to kiss again was like a dying need.

What the fuck is wrong with me?

"You smell like a thunderstorm, like fresh rain and woods, with a hint of orange, like moist earth and warm sun..."

Midnight's eyes fluttered as she stared up at him. "Like the cabin I spent my summers in growing up, before I had Emma..."

Emma... somehow the name struck a chord within Dallas.

"Emma is..." he swallowed nervously.

"My daughter," she whispered, her eyes fluttering shut.

Up close he could smell her intoxicating scent, citrus and vanilla, as she had stated was the scent of most Djinn, but there was something else there. She smelled faintly of cake batter. Like the homemade cakes his wife baked in the early days of her pregnancy.

It made his stomach flip with hunger. He hadn't had cake, especially vanilla cake, in years.

But the admission from her tasty lips froze him in place.

Daughter.

Midnight had a *daughter.*

A thousand questions sped through his brain, but he could not process all of them at the rate they entered his thoughts, and he worried for a moment she could hear him, hear his judgment.

Why did he care what she thought?

It was like whenever he got close enough to her, his walls dropped. The very same walls he'd spent years building, only to let in a select few—Malcolm, Ava, the Goon Squad.

Jake Dallas rarely let anyone into his wasteland, into his inner graveyard, and even those he did let in, it took years to build that level of trust. No one had infiltrated his fortress quite so quickly. He'd barely known Midnight for more than seven days.

And she answered them.

"She was...taken from me. When I was turned. I've been trying to find her, to get her back for four years." Her voice shook, her eyes turning glassy.

Dallas's heart broke, a feat he was more than surprised by. He hadn't thought his heart could break anymore than it had the moment he woke up realizing he was no longer human.

"The Boracellis took her, didn't they?" he asked as all the puzzle pieces fell into place.

Midnight's animosity toward them, her fighting him to try and make it across the border to that dreadful estate.

She nodded as her eyes filled with tears.

"You saved me," she said, her voice faint like a ghost. She slid her right hand up his arm, resting it on his bicep as she caught his gaze once more. Her eyes burned bright like sapphires, and in them he could see a sadness that called to his own.

He'd saved a lot of people since Laura's death. But he'd always regretted leaving for drinks that night because he believed if he hadn't, he would have somehow been able to prevent hers and their daughter's death. He swore he'd do everything over if he had the chance, even the sliver of a chance to save her and Kelly.

Kelly.

Remembering her name brought forth a wave of fresh grief. He'd never gotten the chance to hold her, to see what color eyes she would have had, or if she would have had her mother's smile.

And if he had that chance, and someone *took* her from him... he knew he'd do whatever he could to get her back, too.

And in that one moment, he understood Midnight better than he'd ever understood anyone in his entire life.

Deep inside the coffin that he buried all his trauma, all his wishful thinking, he understood on some imperceptible level that she saw *him* in that moment, and the force between them swelled tenfold. Monster or no monster, there were some things that were transcendent.

Being a parent was one of them.

His breath shook as he realized how close to the edge he was. Of telling her everything, of kissing her, of letting his demons run free, and he pulled away.

Get a hold of yourself, D.

"Now we're even," he said as he took a step away from her, leaving her standing on her own two feet for the moment.

Her eyebrows furrowed and her lip tensed.

"I suppose we are," she said softly.

"Amora said you need to eat," he stated, glazing over the sudden tension that had formed between them. "And quite frankly, as much as I don't want to… I know I need to," he said as he gave her his back.

"I am a little hungry," she said.

He turned for a moment, gathering his sense of self, which seemed to be much more difficult all of a sudden. Usually, he had better control than this. He noted a blush crept into her cheeks, making her look almost… cute. If a woman who looked like Morticia Addams in biker gear could be classified as such.

The fact the sight alone made him wonder what the rest of her body would look like with tinged pink markings, caused his cock to throb. He turned his back once more as he headed for the door, if only to adjust himself and his burgeoning erection that didn't seem to get the memo that now was not the time for fucking.

Especially monsters you're supposed to be taking care of for the moment.

Despite the emotional bombshells.

Though the ache in his loins was fierce, he had to acknowledge the fact it had been over a week since he'd met his end at the Marquis, since he and Ava had made love last. Something that shouldn't have mattered. After all, he'd gone plenty of lengths of time without needing to have sex.

But it seemed now, in this new stronger body, the need was like a dull ache in the background, always there, always pulsing with need along with his hunger.

The memory of Ava filled his psyche with sadness and pain.

He told Ava the truth. That he loved

her, and she hadn't said it back.

And then he'd whisked her away to make love to her in *his* bed, hoping she would understand his actions, hoping in that action that perhaps he'd feel what she couldn't say out loud.

The very same bed in that he hadn't brought any woman home to in sixteen years.

He hadn't even wanted to sleep there himself, knowing all the love and beautiful moments made there with his wife were now just as dead as she was.

It was the only time he and Ava had ever pushed past the heat of their constant battle of dominance, into intimate territory. Sure, they had fucked around enough in motels and bar bathrooms, and once on his motorcycle in the middle of the woods, over the two years they'd been together.

Even if they kept their relationship a secret.

But there was a difference between throwing Ava over his lap and pushing her over the edge until she begged him to let her come, and another for her to *hold* onto him as he filled her, staring into his eyes with unspoken words and emotion she'd buried for two years because she was afraid of letting her walls down, too.

It was the only time Ava had ever truly opened up to him, let him into her heart just a fraction. The weight of such things was not lost on him as he kissed her, as he filled her, his fingertips grazing over her scars where she'd been sliced open by vicious vampires, left to die. Like him, she was a survivor, a fighter. She'd lost so much in her short twenty-two years of life.

He'd had her body for two years, but never her heart.

Every kiss, every touch, every desire, a stolen moment, but that night, just before they'd gotten in the car and taken off for the Marquis, they'd turned a corner into the unknown.

He'd let his guard down completely for the first time as he watched her walls crumble around them, too.

He hadn't realized until they'd both arrived at that pivotal peak, how much he missed feeling *connected* to someone like that.

The thought of fucking anyone else still felt confusing to him. He wasn't ready to let go.

Of Laura, of Ava, of hope.

Old habits, and all.

But Dallas knew there would be no love rekindled with the youngest Crowley, now. No matter how he felt about her.

He could not afford to put her in danger, and he certainly couldn't show up on her doorstep a monster, expecting her to run away with him into the sunset to live happily ever after.

Ava wasn't like that, and he knew that the moment he kissed her in a boxing ring after she'd been bitten. It was one of the reasons he loved her.

You can't get hurt if you have no expectations.

But perhaps somewhere in the last four years, Dallas had forgotten such things. He'd let himself dream, hope, and wish for a future that was never meant to be his, and that would never be now that he was no longer human.

But somewhere in the depths of his dark, tormented soul, the dirt had shifted, the coffin rattled, making way for the seeds of hope to take root once again.

"Let's go, I'm fucking starving," he said as he walked through the door into the night, into the unknown.

12

MIDNIGHT FELT STRANGE. While she had felt the effects of vampire venom before, this time something was different. She'd regained her ability to walk, but she still felt shaky, and the intoxicating thunderstorm scent wafting off of the Djinn beside her was making her dizzy. She shivered as the cool Kentucky air kissed her skin.

Dallas shot her a scathing look.

"It's not even cold out," he grumbled.

"It's freezing out here. How are you not cold?" she bit, eyeing up his shirt turned muscle tank she'd grown used to seeing over the past week. The long sides exposed his muscular torso as well as his defined biceps. The cut outs along the sides cast shadows on his toned abdomen from the nearby streetlamps, and she had to admit it wasn't a terrible look on him, if she was being honest.

That first night she'd taken him back to the Clam after saving him, she had questioned herself multiple times, albeit Rebel had also questioned her sanity, her decision to adopt a feral, unbound Djinn.

"I don't know what you think you're doing, but this is insane even for you," *Rebel said as she followed Midnight*

down to Ami's office. With the cops being all over the Marquis, and the vampires running to the shadows to hide among the patrons who had shown up, it was only a matter of time before Ami and The Heartsgrave would return to the Clam to regroup.

Thankfully, Dallas was not the first rescue she'd seen. Harrison, a ghoul they'd found wasting away on animal carcasses alongside the road near four months ago had been brought into The Heartsgrave and welcomed with open arms, until he'd expired, of course. Ami had even given him fresh clothing.

Clothing she kept in a large rubbermaid container in the storage lockers behind her office in the Clam.

She'd barely noticed anything was missing, Midnight told herself as she punched in the code for the storage room.

"It's seventy four degrees," Dallas deadpanned.

"What are you, a meteorologist?" she nipped as she rubbed her arms. The walk to the Badlands bar seemed to be longer than she anticipated, or perhaps it was because time itself seemed to be slowed down to a crawl since she could barely concentrate on anything except the man beside her.

She had expected to wake up to Rebel, or even Boo as a caretaker, certainly not the lumbering *Viper* beside her.

The more she thought about the name, the more fitting it seemed for him.

"Fucking hell, Midnight, just stop okay?" he said as he removed his tank. She stopped dead in her tracks, noticing the sheen of sweat that sparkled in the moonlight over his chest.

She'd seen glimpses of his pecs through his tank, through his tattered clothes the night she'd found him, but to see Jake Dallas shirtless in front of her, bathed in moonlight, was something else entirely. Midnight couldn't help the heat that flushed through her body at the sight. As her gaze fell on two double star tattoos underneath each of his taut, tan nipples, she was practically salivating, again.

Christ almighty, Midnight, it's not like you've never seen a man chest before, good lord!

He offered her the shirt. *His* shirt.

She looked at it as if it was a literal snake, and reaching for it would only end in losing her limb.

"You're hot," she said dumbfounded. At the realization of her words, she immediately tried to cover up how desperate she sounded.

"I mean, you are sweating..." She cleared her throat as she took the shirt from his hands. It was warm to the touch, and comforted her just a fraction. Without thinking, she clutched it in her fist, breathing in Dallas's warm, heady scent. If he noticed, he didn't dwell on her strange behavior.

"Yeah, I've uh... kind of been burning up since I killed that vampire," he said.

Midnight slid the tank over top of her own, wrapping the large shirt around her like a jacket. In comparison, it was pretty large for her frame. Instinct overcame her as she took a step forward. Maybe she wasn't the only one who had sustained injuries. Men were less likely to talk about being hurt, monster or no monster.

"Are you hurt?" she asked calmly as she approached him.

Dallas did not move, but his gaze held hers.

"I'm fine." he said.

Midnight twisted her lips.

"Are you absolutely sure? If you've been hurt somehow, you need to tell me." She looked up at him, imploring him with her eyes to trust her. Something told her such a thing was not easy for him.

Trust.

She was about to give up, about to turn around and head back toward the Badlands when he spoke.

"I think one of the wolves nipped me,

but it's nothing."

Midnight's heart sank.

"A werewolf bit you? Are you sure?" she asked, pulling his warm tank tighter around her arms, her muscles tensing.

"I mean, I was a bit... busy to take numbers but... yeah, just a scratch. Nothing to worry about. I've had a lot worse," he said.

"I don't think it meant to, either. It just... sort of happened in the madness, you know."

"That explains the sweating..." she murmured as she stepped closer. She approached Dallas as one would approach a literal snake, calmly, slowly.

"It does?" Dallas deadpanned.

Midnight nodded.

"Wolves naturally run hot. Higher metabolisms, more energy. Being bit by one won't kill you, but you'll probably experience some of the basic wolf... stuff."

Dallas's jaw tensed.

"Like..."

"Body temp rising, instinct or desire to just... say what you think without warning, act on... impulse." She swallowed nervously.

"We call it... Scratch Fever."

Dallas huffed in annoyance.

"You can't be serious."

Midnight placed her hand on his chest, half expecting him to shove her away but he didn't. She let her palm settle over his heart, her fingers brushing the hard, muscle, sliding across the smoothness of his sweat-slicked skin. She stilled her hand, feeling the vibration of his heart beating beneath her fingers.

His blue eyes glowed, and the scent of thunderstorms and rain filled her airways. It was impossible to resist, and so she couldn't help when she took a deep inhale, before speaking.

"Heartbeat's a little rapid. That's classic werewolf," she said, her voice much darker than it should have been. She swallowed nervously.

"Wolf saliva isn't as toxic as vamp venom, but then again vamp venom attacks the body. Wolf saliva attacks your brain, your impulse control, but you're, uh... a big guy, so my guess is you should burn through it in about twenty-four hours or so..." She said the words as she focused on the feel of his skin, of the warmth emanating from his body. It was like she was absorbing his warmth, feeling it spread throughout her entire being, culminating in her core. The spark of electricity as she touched him lit her insides up like a powder keg, causing a surprise wetness to bloom between her thighs. Her own breath started to come in rapid succession with Dallas's chaotic heartbeat. Suddenly, Midnight was feeling a bit feverish herself.

"Where?" she asked, much huskier than she'd intended.

"Where did you get bit?"

"My ankle. But like I said, it's fine." His gaze caught hers, holding it for a moment before his voice deepened, causing another flutter in her groin.

"I promise, I'm fine. You don't need to worry about me. I'm not the one who needs *supervision* right now, Bambi."

Something about his words soothed her anxiety for the moment, as she stared back in his venetian blue eyes. Without thinking, she smacked him, noting the twitch in his lips that looked almost like a… smile.

"Fine. But I swear, if you start wolfing out on me…"

"What? What are *you* going to do?" He snickered, licking his bottom lip, his blue eyes glazing over with mischief. She could feel the steam practically building between them.

Before Midnight could answer, he shook his head, the smile that ghosted across his face gone in a flash.

"Now, if you're done pissing around out here, I'd like us to make it to the damn bar before last call."

Midnight nodded in response.

ARIEL DAWN

"Of course, lead the way, Jake."

***

The Badlands wasn't much different than the array of other bars Midnight had been in over the course of the past four years. After all, you've seen one dive bar, you've seen them all. But it wasn't the crowd or the ever-flowing liquor that stirred her insides with hope, with need.

It was the stage in which someone was currently belting out *I Will Always Love You* in a key that should have only been performed for deaf dogs.

Midnight realized that Dallas was still shirtless, and she slowly pulled his shirt off of her, feeling an emptiness when she was no longer wearing it. She tapped him on the shoulder, and he nearly jumped five feet off the ground.

"You, uh... should probably take this," she said as she held it out. Dallas's eyes glowed bright like neon, brighter than she'd ever seen them.

He shook his head.

"I don't need it," he said with a grunt. Despite the clarity of his voice, she could see the hunger in his eyes.

"You okay?" she asked, if only because she knew the answer. She just wasn't sure if despite their pow-wow in Boo's motel room if he was ready to let her in. If he was ready to trust her.

"I just... uh... it's noisy."

The chatter in the bar wasn't abnormal. A group of men played pool in the corner, and the dance floor in front of the wailing karaoke king was populated enough with men and women booing and cheering, not to mention the bar was packed with patrons drinking, talking, laughing.

Music filled the air, and so did the scent of sweet liquor. Midnight's stomach flipped, and she couldn't help but lick her lips.

The place was full of hopes and dreams, tonight.

But it wasn't the populous chatter Dallas was talking about. Instinctively, Midnight reached her hand out, taking his.

Dallas's entire body tensed and she could feel that same bolt of lightning she felt when she'd touched him earlier, shooting through her body like a comet, lighting up all the forgotten parts of her.

She ran her thumb smoothly over his knuckle.

"I hear them, too, you know. But you

can tune them out. Set the noise to a faint hum."

"How?" he asked, his palm sweaty against hers.

"Simple. You find something to focus on. A target, a thought, an action."

"You telling me all I have to do is think about something else? Don't you think I *want* to think about something other than fucking blood and sex?" He growled. His cheeks flushed immediately at his freudian slip. He dropped her hand.

Midnight smirked.

"Maybe you just need a drink to relax. You seem tense."

Dallas shed his unnatural air of concern, trading it for one that wasn't quite as endearing. The persona Midnight was used to.

Smart as a tack, sharp witted.

Cocky, arrogant.

"It's been a rough fucking week."

"What's your poison?" she asked as she headed for the bar.

"I've never been particularly picky. Whatever is on tap is fine with me."

"Really? I would have pegged you for a whiskey man," she said as she sidled up to the bar, sliding between two men. Dallas tailed behind her, keeping a modicum of space between them, yet she could still feel his presence looming over her like some knight in shining armor.

Though Midnight knew Jake Dallas was the furthest thing from a fairytale, but that only intrigued her more.

"Well, hello there..." One of the men noticed as she slid between them, and immediately she could feel his hope, his lustful wishing as she leaned over the bar bumper, signaling for the bartender.

She ignored him. But it seemed that would not do.

"Hey, sweetheart, I'm talking to you," the man nipped.

Midnight did not give him the time of day.

The bartender came over almost immediately.

Midnight wasted no time ordering their drinks, just as the man grabbed her by the waist, jostling her around, the motion jarring to her already shaky frame. She nearly upended herself into his lap.

Nearly.

For the flash of hot, sweat-slicked skin appeared before her in an instant.

"I don't think the lady wants to talk to

you, pal," Dallas growled, his voice edged on something much darker, much more sinister than the playful tone he'd had before they walked into the bar.

"Viper…" she whispered, setting her hand on his bicep. In public, it was easier to use their code names, after all most of The Heartsgrave had been left for dead, which meant more than half of them were technically reported as dead.

Though it wasn't an obvious chance they could be seen or recognized, using their club names worked easier. Midnight had meant every word she said. The new name made leaving an old life behind much easier.

Midnight watched as the man's face turned bright pink.

"Can't you feel his *wishful thinking…*" she purred. Something shifted in

Dallas's eyes as her words hit him.

He turned to look at her for a moment, nodding the slightest movement.

"Don't take it personally, Don Juan, you aren't my type," Dallas grumbled as he shoved the man off his barstool.

The man didn't waste a second as he swung at Dallas, who didn't even have to move for the man to miss.

Dallas stopped him with a hand in the air. The man tried to throw punches at Dallas but it was no use.

Midnight set her hand on his hip, whispering in his ear.

"Just open your mouth. You don't need to bite, just... focus. On his energy, on his wishful thoughts..." Her breath caught in her throat. Dallas's smooth, warm skin lulled her into her own trance as her eyelashes fluttered, as she coaxed the lumbering hunter through the process.

"Don't fight it," she whispered. She could feel Dallas's entire being tense and so she set her other hand on his hip, massaging his side sweetly.

"Focus on his thoughts... of me," she instructed.

Dallas grimaced, biting his lip.

The faint smell of iron filled her nostrils.

Blood.

Dallas's blood smelled delectable, like warm, raspberry pie.

And with those words, the images assaulted Midnight.

The man's hand on her ass, and his thoughts of buying her a drink or two or three, enough until she'd gotten sloppy enough he could coerce her for a quickie in the bathroom.

Dallas's body shook against her, his temperature rising.

Give him what he wants... focus on his energy and build his image in your mind.

She hadn't meant to mindspeak, and until this moment she had thought the earlier mindspeak incident was isolated.

But Dallas's consciousness was open, responding to her of its own accord.

What if I don't want to give him what he wants?

His voice in her head sounded possessive, commanding. It stirred up that familiar heat, the fire inside of Midnight she'd thought had died with her ex.

Feeding was a mutual, intimate thing for a Djinn. While most preferred to use their fangs and drink down blood, Midnight had found channeling the wishful thinking itself in those moments of inebriation, in the moments where humans felt alive, challenged, was just as divine as any wishes fulfilled by blood consumption.

"You need to eat, too. A hunter can't live without its prey."

Midnight felt a strange sense of energy overcome her, one full of lust. Of dirty thoughts and impulses, and she couldn't quite garner if it was Dallas's strange behavior or the magical connection that seemed to exist between them. The mindspeak, the little sparks when they touched.

Feeling Dallas's hunger, his desire to consume and protect like it was a part of her.

Dallas opened his mouth to speak, but thought better of it. Instead, he focused on the man in front of him. It didn't take long for the man's aura to start colorizing, to materialize in front of them. As his red aura ebbed, his color drained from his face.

To the regular mortal, no one would notice the glowing aura or the transference happening. They'd only see what they wanted to see, if they noticed anything at all.

Dallas dropped the man, who fell to the floor in a heap, dazed and confused.

Midnight rubbed his hips gently, if only to soothe the panic she could feel through the strange bond that she'd somehow formed with the man in front of her.

"You did what you needed to do, and

no one got hurt," she purred in his ear, willing him with a charm all her own to accept this new reality once and for all.

While other Djinn like Enchantress and Rebel, among others, preferred to drain their victims until their last drop, Midnight knew that life itself was precious. She'd spent four years only taking what she needed to get by, because to her there were more important things than blood and the things it carried.

Just because she was a monster, did not mean she had to act like one.

Above all else, she desired to be a woman worthy of Emma.

Something good, even in a monstrous form.

Dallas turned around in her grasp as the man on the floor stumbled to stand, mumbling something incoherent before walking away and leaving them in peace. Dallas's bright eyes gazed down at her, his irises rimmed with fresh red aura haze. The look on his face caused Midnight's entire body to flourish with heat, just as it had in Boo's motel room.

The magnetic pull was strong, but Midnight couldn't tell if it was because he had just eaten, if it was a side effect of his wolf bite, or if it was just the unwavering attraction of Dallas's bad boy hunter vibe, but she felt bewitched by the man and all that he was at that moment.

Dallas set his large hands on her hips, yanking her closer.

Midnight's heart fluttered. The scent of thunderstorms and rain soothed her soul, and she took a deep breath, letting it fill her lungs.

"Thank you," he whispered, bringing his lips to her ear. The heat of his breath on her skin caused goosebumps to prickle her skin, caused her breath to hitch. She fell into his grasp like a fawning lamb.

The aura of Jake Dallas was more than difficult to ignore, and made her hungry, too.

"Don't mention it," she whispered back.

"Hey, lovebirds, your drinks are up," the bartender snipped, breaking whatever spell had fallen over them.

Midnight gently extricated herself from Dallas's grip, despite the fact she didn't want to. But now was not the time for such things.

Just as Dallas picked up his drink,

the doors behind them opened, the familiar scent of wet dog wafting in with the sudden surprise.

Midnight turned, glass in hand, her gaze falling on a group of men and women who all looked similar in their appearance. Large, like Dallas, with muscles for days, tan skin, dark eyes and hair, and all in various flannel prints and colors and ripped jeans. The temperature of the room rose, like a fanning fire.

"Do you smell that?" Midnight asked, her blood running cold.

Dallas turned, beer in hand and a scowl on his face.

"Looks like we have company," he grumbled.

Midnight clutched her drink a little tighter, as the pack of werewolves scattered, one of them headed directly over to where they were, his eyes focused on Midnight and Dallas.

"Drink up Jake, I think we're in for a long night."

13

DALLAS TENSED IMMEDIATELY upon seeing the group of individuals who had entered the bar. While he'd always had a bit of preternatural sense as a human, it seemed that as a Djinn, the same instinctual awareness was now much more intense.

He'd been hunting monsters for years, and while most of his experience was relative to vampires, demons, ghosts, and possessed individuals, he had encountered werewolves before, two years prior. Though he hadn't seen any since, not until he'd arrived in Mayfield, when he and Midnight had gone to canvas the area of Amora's orders.

But Dallas didn't need years of experience to know the men and women in front of him were werewolves. Every hair on his body stood, his blood reacting on some undistinguishable level. While he'd never been one to fear monsters in their entirety, something about this group, this *pack,* made him feel a sense of caution, and immediately without thinking he stood in front of Midnight, his shoulders tensing, his eyes narrowing.

He locked eyes on one man in particular, one who stood in front, dressed in dark blue flannel and a black shirt, his blondish-brown hair almost like spun gold against the deep tan color of his skin. And he was walking straight toward Dallas, flanked by another man who looked eerily similar in design, the only difference was the color of his eyes, and his dark hair, not to mention he was wearing a black shirt with a tear in it.

"Well, well, what do we have here?" the blue-flannel wolf said as he approached Dallas.

"We don't want any trouble," Midnight said as she stepped around him, causing his insides to flare up with panic.

Dallas cast her a look that spoke volumes, but Midnight did not seem to care.

"We're just here to enjoy ourselves a

drink or two like everyone else."

Her voice was smooth, gentle. It carried an innocence that both flared his protective nature and also eased his own stress.

The wolf in blue flannel smirked at her, the sight causing Dallas's blood to boil

Mine.

The stray thought pushed through his mind like a ricocheting bullet.

In all reality, Dallas knew he didn't *own* anyone. He hadn't owned Laura, or Ava, and he certainly didn't have any claim to Midnight. But despite knowing such things, he couldn't deny the irrefutable truth in the word as he thought it.

It felt more right than it should have.

But Dallas didn't have time to ponder

on such things. He stood straighter, flexing his muscles as he cracked his knuckles, letting this pain in the ass wolf know he would fight if he needed to. The man did not seem to care.

"Not too often we see your kind around here," the man spoke, his voice edged in warning.

"And just exactly what *kind* are you referring to?" Dallas pulled back his lips in a snarl of his own, showcasing his newfound fangs.

"Oh, I think we both know what *kind* I am referring to," the man said as he signaled the bartender, who stepped over immediately.

The other man who was with him set a hand on blue flannel wolf's shoulder, his eyes meeting Dallas's. There was something oddly familiar about his golden eyes...

"We don't want any trouble either, do we, Thomas?" the man in the black shirt spoke, his voice deeper, more refined. The one in blue spoke with an accent that Dallas was certain had to be regional, as it sounded all too similar to the one the desk attendant had.

Thomas looked between Dallas and Midnight, just as black shirt spoke again.

"After all, this is the man who saved my life today."

Dallas's blood chilled as memories flooded him of the fray that had landed him with a wolf bite on his ankle.

"You..." he started to speak as black shirt extended his hand.

"It's Alaric, actually. Alaric Thorne."

Dallas looked at Alaric's hand,

contemplating for a moment if it was some sort of trap.

The softest touch of fingertips on his hip soothed him almost instantly, almost as if the touch alone could cut through the fog that had befallen him.

Dallas was acutely aware that Tom was watching him, judging him.

So he slowly reached out and took Alaric's hand, shaking it firmly if only to tell this wolf that he, too, was a force to be reckoned with.

Alaric shook, his grip tight before he dropped it.

"Thanks, man," Alaric said with a firm nod.

Thomas grabbed a beer from the bartender, handing it to Alaric before taking his own.

"Don't mention it," Dallas said as he

turned around to face Midnight.

"We should get out of here," he said, his voice solid and unwavering; carefully covering up the rush of anxiety swelling within him.

"We just got here," she said, squeezing his side lightly.

"At least let me buy you a drink?" Alaric said, pulling his attention away.

"Not every day I get my ass saved by a Djinn."

Dallas looked between Midnight and Alaric, noticing Tom's expression of disdain. Alaric must have caught on, as he set his hand on Dallas's shoulder.

"Don't worry about him, his bark is worse than his bite. It's an alpha thing," Alaric said with a smirk.

Something in the wolf's smile, in his demeanor, set Dallas at ease. He wasn't attacking, and for the moment it seemed a truce had been drawn.

"Fine," he said. "One drink."

***

"You've got to be kidding me!" Alaric barked as he slammed down his shot glass. The entirety of the Mayfield pack had practically taken over the Badlands, as Dallas had learned Thomas Mayfield himself owned it.

He found that Alaric, alpha of the Thorne pack, was assisting his fellow friend with the sudden influx of blood suckers.

Apparently, they'd be trying to catch the vamps themselves, but up until earlier that night, when their paths had crossed, they hadn't been successful in getting a look or survey of the estate they were occupying.

The fray hadn't been for nothing. Alaric reported due to the distraction—and the Djinn"s help, Dallas included—they'd discovered several hostages, including a small group of children.

Dallas found it easy to talk to Alaric, but he wasn't sure if that was because of who Alaric was as a person, or if it had to do with the three glasses of beer, and four shots he'd had.

Midnight slammed down her shot glass, smiling sweetly.

"Read 'em and weep, wolf," she said with a giggle as Alaric slapped a small wad of bills on the bar.

"Well earned, miss Midnight," Alaric said.

The last notes of *Shook Me All Night Long* ended as one of the pack members climbed off the stage.

"I'm going up," Midnight said, her voice determined.

Dallas rolled his eyes.

"What?" she said as she pushed away from the table.

"I didn't say anything!" Dallas said in defense, putting his hands in the air.

Alaric laughed.

"You didn't have to," Midnight said as she sauntered to where he sat.

"The stage is that way, Bambi," he said cockily as he waved his arms to the side, his gaze catching hers.

She smirked, her own blue eyes glazed from the copious amounts of liquor they'd been drinking.

"Please, I've seen the way *you've* been eyeing up that mic. You can have fun, too, you know. It's not illegal."

Dallas bit his tongue. It was true he'd been watching the droves of karaoke participants, some pack members, some not, which was easily distinguishable from their golden skin and stocky, flannel covered frames. Most of them probably couldn't carry a tune when they were sober.

Watching them sing haphazardly along to the classics he grew up loving so much was damn near torture, and made him realize how much he not only missed Mal and the other hunters, but how much he missed their band, Blood Of My Enemy.

It wasn't all that long ago, that they were in a bar much like this one, doing nearly the same thing.

Mal would undoubtedly drink too much, Tito would swindle some poor asshole out of a good chunk of change playing pool, Hunter would get wasted and drone on about tomes and lore, and Vinny... well, Vinny usually kept to himself most of the time, content to have a beer or two, and just enjoy being in everyone's presence.

And Dallas would always find some beautiful woman to serenade in the crowd, who he'd undoubtedly crawl into bed with. And on the nights they got the band together to play, Dallas loved every minute of it. It was often him who booked them the gigs they played.

His smile faltered as he wondered what would become of the band now that he was... indisposed.

Would they continue performing without him?

Find someone else to replace him?

The thought caused his heart to twist in pain. He hated the idea of the band going on without him, but it was more than that and he knew it. He hated the idea that his family—the only one he had left—lived without him.

"I know how to have fun, Midnight," he grumbled.

"I wasn't fucking born yesterday."

"Then get up there. We can make it fun. I'll let you pick my song," she said with a wink.

Against the light of the bar, her dark hair spilling over her shoulders, she looked endearing. She also seemed a bit more at ease, happier almost. But Dallas knew that was likely the alcohol talking, and a part of him wanted to see her botch the performance, just so he could tease her about it. Watch her get all worked up, watch her fair cheeks stain with angry blush.

A slow smile spread across Dallas's face. Maybe he could have a little fun.

"All right. One song," he said as he got up and followed her to the stage. When he saw her climb the stairs, he leaned over and told the DJ his song choice.

He smirked as the first lines of Paula Abdul's *Cold Hearted* came over the speakers, expecting Midnight to falter. After all, it wasn't as popular as Paula Abdul's *Straight Up*, which in his experience, meant most people didn't know it.

But Midnight only smiled and shook her head. And when she opened her mouth to sing the opening words, *"He's a cold-hearted snake,"* something magical happened.

Dallas stood below the stage, and he could not take his eyes off of her.

Midnight grabbed the microphone, her long fingers curled around its base, her voice like a siren's. It was crisp, clear, smooth like brandy and warm like a hot summer night. With nothing but a microphone to hold, Midnight *owned* the stage. The energy in the room shifted completely, and he could see emerging auras in the crowd, almost as if they were being sucked into her siren vortex.

She's feeding.

He realized all of a sudden, the fractured memories of his life since awakening mingling with her words, that perhaps feeding didn't have to be a fight, a frenzy.

Like he had consumed the energy of

the asshole who'd dared to *touch* her when she was more than clear she wanted nothing to do with him, he realized that perhaps there was a way he could live with what he now needed.

And for the glimmer of a moment, Dallas dared to wish, to hope that in the ashes of his death he could live again.

That he didn't have to hurt anyone again.

And at that moment, Midnight caught his gaze. Amidst the lights shining down on her, he could see her aura glowing, all shades of blue and purple like the milky way galaxy.

The world around him fell away, until there was nothing but the sound of her voice, the sparkle in her eyes, and the beat of his heart in his chest reminding him he was alive.

He was *alive.*

And when Midnight finished singing, the crowd roaring with applause, she bounded down the steps, her foot catching on the last one, nearly causing her to fall.

But Dallas was right there.

He moved with precision, quickly, instinctively. Midnight would never touch the ground, he'd make sure of it.

She fell into his arms like rain falls on the tin roof, droplets of water sliding down against the cool metal in slow motion. He righted her, the heat between them blossoming like an orchid in dark, uninhabitable places.

"It's your turn," she whispered, her bright eyes staring back at him, and it was like she truly saw *him.* Saw through the rough armor and exterior, past his sarcasm and pain, the things he dared not speak, and the ghosts he could not seem to let go of.

And when her fingertips squeezed his bicep, her lips parted as her breath hitched, Dallas knew he needed to get on stage.

If he didn't he might do something he regretted.

"Right," he said as he removed his arms from around her, hating how empty and cold he felt without Midnight's body to warm him, to soothe his inner storms.

Dallas climbed the stage, the lights blinding. He looked out into the sea of people, feeling the effects of his liquor. When the beginning notes of *Heaven Is A Place On Earth* started to play, Dallas couldn't help but laugh.

Of course, you'd pick something like this... fuck.

But he wasn't about to throw in the towel now, no.

He had braved so much in his long thirty-five years of life, surely he could handle a little pop song.

Dallas took one look at the crowd, noting their auras were still glowing, hungry for more of what Midnight had given them. And in that moment, he knew he would deliver. It was like a switch had been flipped.

The show must go on.

He grabbed his microphone, commanding the stage as he always did when he sung along with his friends during their gigs.

"Oh baby, do you know what that's worth?" he crooned, his stance shifting

as he tapped his foot along with the beat. The lights shone on him as he found his rhythm, moving his body in a way he hadn't in quite awhile.

It'd been a long time since Jake Dallas *danced.* Since he'd wanted to.

"Baby, I was afraid, before, but I'm not afraid, anymore." He sang the words as they filled him with a vibrant energy. His voice was as strong as it always was when he performed, and when he looked out into the crowd, he only saw bright blue eyes full of excitement and praise, and crimson tinged cheeks, and he couldn't resist smiling. The melodic, upbeat lyrics had a power all their own, begging to be sung from his whole heart. Under the lights of the stage he felt alive, and warm.

For the first time in a long time,

Dallas felt *free.*

He belted out the lyrics with ease, despite his alcohol consumption, and swallowed down the wishful thoughts, the energy the crowd fed him. Aura's glowed in his eyesight, fractals of energy dancing in the air, feeding a hunger in him he hadn't realized existed until this moment. And it wasn't just their wishful thoughts, their hopes and dreams that fed him, no.

It was the feeling he always got performing in front of a crowd. And just when he expected the song to be cut short, it went on.

Oh shit, it's the extended version.

However unprepared, he recuperated quickly, working the crowd in the bar like he would have if he was performing metal covers. He clapped his hands, motioning for the crowd to follow along, and as their auras, their wishful thoughts and dreams fed him, they did as he asked.

They clapped, they sang.

Heat ransacked him and he didn't think twice about running his hand through his wet hair, which elicited more than a few howls from the audience. He smirked at the crowd's response, his skin glistening in the harsh stage light, muscles and tattoos on full display.

And when he fell to his knees for his big finish, rippling his muscles and casting a cocky smile at a blushing Midnight, the energy in the room flared.

Midnight *glowed*, her own bluish purple aura brighter than anything else.

Just as the song ended, the doors opened, and the energy in the room shifted to make way for Amora and her band of misfit toys. Thomas stood up immediately from his seat, and the pack turned their heads in their direction.

"Well, I do love a good pomp and circumstance, but there is no need. I come in peace," Amora said as she held her hands up in front of herself.

Boo and Rebel flanked her, the rest of The Heartsgrave looking a bit grim, even for monsters.

Dallas was frozen. He watched from the stage as Thomas and Amora took ten paces toward one another, like Godzilla was getting ready to take on Mothra.

Though he wasn't quite certain who was Godzilla.

"And what do you come for, *Your Highness*?" Thomas sneered.

Amora cocked her head to the side.

"I come to propose an alliance," Amora said.

"Fuck," Dallas breathed.

Thomas and Amora stared at each other for a moment before he nodded.

"Let us discuss this matter privately, then," he said.

The collective energy in the room was full of relief. There would be no bloodshed here, tonight, it seemed.

Dallas set his microphone down, as he bounded down the steps to Midnight, who looked a little pale.

"I think that's our cue, Bambi."

14

MIDNIGHT WALKED ACROSS the parking lot, Dallas tailing behind her.

Her entire body flushed with heat, both in part to the alcohol she'd consumed—which she noted as her stomach flipped upside down, was probably not a good mix in retrospect with the vampire venom making its way through her system—and the show Dallas had put on back in The Badlands.

She hadn't expected him to utterly kill the sugary eighties song quite like he had. And when he'd dropped to his knees, shirtless, sliding his hand down his rock-hard abs toward his...

Stop it, Midnight. You can't go there. You absolutely can't. The last time you fell for the bad boy, you ended up pregnant.

Midnight sighed, her thoughts conflicting. While she hadn't regretted having Emma, she did regret everything that had transpired between her and Trevor. She'd fallen into Trevor's web of deceit, believed him and all his lies. He was charming, after all, and mysterious. An outsider on the run.

Midnight was stuck. She was stuck in her small town, serving stale coffee and pie at the Starlight Diner to those who just happened to pass through her hometown of Burlington, New Jersey.

So naturally, the pale-skinned, rogue snake charmer that Trevor was appealed to her. His white-toothed smile and smoldering eyes mixed with his saccharine compliments and a natural air of attraction that surrounded him, should have been her first indication he wasn't like her.

He wasn't human.

Even now as she walked at a brisk pace through the parking lot, the chill air on her skin, she hated that her thoughts strayed to *him,* to the night that changed her life.

She'd gone over it a hundred times, a thousand times, probably.

How he'd slid his hand over hers when she set his pie down. How he'd flashed his amber eyes at her, how they glowed and her entire body felt warm like melted chocolate.

The haze that fell over her as he asked if she wanted to play a little game.

Midnight had never been an impulsive person until that day. Despite her outward appearance, she was the epitome of a good girl. She never broke the rules.

But when Trevor Boracelli spoke, she felt inclined to do whatever he asked, almost as if she was *compelled* to do so. Though she thought at least he'd let her take him *home* to fuck.

But Trevor didn't want to wait. His impulsivity was one of the things she'd admired about him, even when they'd been together for those short, few years.

The diner bathroom door had barely

locked before he had her panties around her ankles, her uniform skirt rumpled at the small of her back. The air of danger and excitement melded together with the feel of his cool skin against her back as Trevor wasted no time fitting himself inside of her.

Somewhere in her mind, she knew she should say no. To him, to the situation.

For starters, she never let any man come near her without a condom, not to mention she knew the rules about fraternizing with customers and other employees, especially on the clock. But it was as if the walls she'd carefully constructed had been completely annihilated, and for the first time in her short twenty-five years of life, she felt free.

Free to be the person she always *wished* she could be.

Spontaneous, alive for the moment instead of calculating and anxious.

She hadn't disliked the rush that came with Trevor's gorgeous smile, or the reality that despite the door being locked, someone could discover them. The thought caused her loins to throb with desire all the more.

Trevor filled every part of her being, her mind, her soul, her body with life, in more ways than one. Until that moment, Midnight felt like she'd been living some lie. That under his ministrations, the velveteen drag of his cock through her wet folds, she was finally *free* to give in to the deep desire to be someone else. Not the girl who followed the rules, did as she was told, but the one who let hot strangers rail her while telling her she was *such a good girl at taking his cock* at two o'clock on a Sunday afternoon in the employee bathroom. The rattle of the sink as he thrust into her, harder and faster, without care, their heavy breathing, echoed in the caverns of her mind.

And then it was over. When he was finished with her, she could feel the remains of his release dripping down her thighs, and she froze as the high of the moment came crashing down. She barely registered the door opening and closing.

"Midnight!" Dallas called, and she jumped. He motioned to the motel in front of them, which she hadn't even realized they had arrived at. She was practically running for the woods.

"There a fire I don't know about?" Dallas grumbled as he approached her.

The smell of rain and thunderstorms rolled off of him like a tsunami, blanketing her senses.

He smelled *divine*.

Like the sweet summer of home.

Instinctively, his scent flared a hurricane in her stomach. Or perhaps, it was the mixture of venom and tequila. She took a deep breath, letting his intoxicating scent fill her lungs once more. In Dallas's presence, it was hard to resist. Especially when he looked at her, shirtless, with those glowing eyes of blue fire.

"I just... lost track of—"

Dallas cocked his head to the side, raising an eyebrow.

"You're glowing... red," he said with

confusion.

While Djinn needed to see auras as a precaution for consuming wishful thoughts and energy, she knew it was damn near impossible for Djinn to be able to detect other Djinn's auras.

The only case she'd ever heard of was that of Djinn who were bound to one another, and she knew Dallas was not bound to anyone.

His maker had died.

He was, in all sense and shapes, a rogue Djinn.

Like her.

Despite trying to make things work with Emma's father, he'd never bitten her and claimed her as his mate. He never even acted as if he was hungry for her blood, despite being a vampire, and their romantic liaisons dwindled ostensibly after she'd given birth to Emma, something that she'd felt guilty for. But Trevor was not a stable person, having been on the run from his family for nearly a decade.

And when they'd been attacked by the Djinn in the woods on that fateful day, when she'd *lost* Emma...

She'd managed to kill her assailant before she completely blacked out. She hadn't known her attacker was a fabled Djinn. Until Trevor told her the truth about *what* he was, she hadn't even known vampires or monsters existed. And she certainly would not have believed he would have fallen victim to a Djinn, of all monsters.

A Djinn hired by the Boracellis to take back what they felt rightfully belonged to them.

"I'm fine," she said as she turned away from him, just in time to see a man walking toward them from the lobby. A part of her wanted to tell Dallas everything. To let go of the heavy burden she carried with her all the time.

Tell him the truth about Emma, about how a vampire broke her heart, gave their daughter away, and tried to have her killed.

But Midnight could never tell anyone the truth. That she knew Trevor was dangerous, and she'd forced her way into his life, hoping with a baby they could settle down and have a nice, quiet life together, away from the monsters that chased him. Just the three of them, in the woods, raising their beautiful daughter together.

And that wish, that dream, was what

she held onto.

Emma deserves a father, a family.

As always, the words caught in her throat. She'd wanted to say them so many times to Boo and Rebel, even Amora when she'd learned of the woman's disdain for the Boracellis.

While Boo and Rebel knew she was trying to rescue Emma, no one in The Heartsgrave pressed for the root of why *anyone* was there, or what drove them. They knew better. But there had been plenty of times Midnight *wanted* to divulge the truth. Some days it felt like it was eating her alive, to not be able to say Trevor's name out loud.

Trevor Boracelli.

The Boracellis had ruined her life, but they'd also given her her greatest gift. But Emma was more than just a child of a monster.

"You lie like a damn rug," Dallas drawled.

The pain and anxiety of memories Midnight *wished* she could forget swelled within her. No matter how badly she wished she could forget, that she could erase Trevor from her mind, she knew he never would leave, and she hated that. Even in death, he had a grip on her, and she'd always have a piece of him as long as she had Emma.

The best parts of him.

"What does it matter to *you?*" she bit, noting the flash of energy in Dallas's eyes as she did so. She expected him to bite back, quip some douchey comment at her, or just all out be an ass, true to his Viper name, but Dallas did none of those things.

His gaze roved over her and heat enveloped her.

It was only then she realized she was freezing.

The desk attendant stopped just in front of them.

"I, uh... hate to break up this little shindig, but umm, Mr. Dallas, due to an inability to process your information, I'm afraid your reservation has been cancelled."

Dallas's shoulders stiffened as he tore his gaze away from Midnight.

Her heart sunk.

"I—"

"You need to collect your things as soon as possible and vacate the premises, or I will have to contact the authorities," the concierge said, his voice cracking. Nervous energy swelled off of him in droves, and Midnight could not help herself.

"You can stay with me," she said impulsively.

The concierge looked between them. "Uh..."

"There won't be any problem, then, will there? Mr. Dallas can collect his things, you don't have to call any authorities..."

Midnight flashed her gaze at Dallas who was clenching his jaw.

"It's the least I can do," she said honestly.

He'd done his part. He watched over her, fed her, and defended her against that asshole who wouldn't take no for an answer. He'd even been a good sport about the karaoke.

The concierge who knew when to say

when, graciously nodded in approval.

"Yes, that would be fine. However, your room is only one Queen, Miss Rainier." The concierge cleared his throat. He pronounced her last name like the cherry, though it was actually pronounced like the weather.

"I'll figure something out, Midnight, don't worry about it," Dallas said, his shoulders tensing.

Midnight shook her head.

"It's fine, Dallas. Don't worry about it. We're both adults. I don't bite, I promise."

The flush of crimson in Dallas's cheeks would have been funny or cute if he was not also currently shirtless. His reaction caused a small smile to form on her lips. To think the lumbering tower of sex appeal in front of her would *blush* at all, especially over something so trivial, was somehow endearing.

And it only increased her internal hurricane.

It wasn't often Midnight made a man—any man truly—blush.

Not that there have been many in my life to begin with, and definitely not since I gave birth to Emma.

Before she could speak, Dallas crossed his arms in front of his chest, the motion pushing his pecs together and making it hard not to stare.

Midnight fought to keep her gaze on his face, fought to keep all thoughts of running her nails across his taut, hard muscles to herself.

Get a fucking grip, Midnight!

"You need rest. Besides, we both won't fit."

"I can have a cot delivered to your room, if you'd like," the concierge said, also blushing.

"Yeah, that's fine. Do that," Dallas said, speaking up. His voice was stern, commanding, and made Midnight's heart skip a beat.

"Very well, then. I'll have that sent over immediately with your things," the concierge said as he skittered off to make the accommodations.

Midnight propped her hand on her hip, scoffing as she headed for the row of rooms where hers was.

Dallas followed behind, leaving a wide breadth between them.

"Unbelievable," she murmured feeling a bit antsy.

Dallas followed her without question.

"I'm not sleeping with you," he said

brusquely.

Midnight rolled her eyes.

"Wow, you really know how to kill a girl's self-esteem, don't you?" she nipped.

"Midnight..." Dallas growled, his energy flaring between them like a sonar of anger.

"Well, when you wake up with a bad back, don't bitch," she said as she removed her card from her pocket. She did not miss how her hands trembled as she slid the keycard in.

Why am I so nervous? It's not like we're doing anything other than sleeping until the afternoon, anyway, bad backs aside.

Realistically, Amora was more than capable of gallivanting around in the daylight as one of the few vampires left who were of original, powerful coven bloodlines.

Like the rest of The Heartsgrave, Amora did not share details about how she'd come to be the rogue leader of a band of Djinn, though Midnight knew she was once married to a powerful, old coven-blood vampire. Like most alliances at that time, it was arranged, and common knowledge. The alliance had made her a bonafide *Queen,* but Queens did not leave their thrones to play in the dirt with lesser supernaturals unless something—or someone—pushed them out to the edges.

Unless they ran away.

But Midnight would not ask questions. Heartsgrave code, and all.

In nature to their jobs honeytrapping mortals for both their own gain, and

Amora, the Djinn operated mostly at night, as did the vampires.

The sun would be up soon enough, and as Midnight opened the door, she felt a wave of exhaustion overcome her. She sauntered in, leaving the door open for Dallas, not even bothering to look at him as she made a beeline for the shower. She realized upon entering the room she felt rather sticky and sweaty from their trip to The Badlands.

"All I'm saying is... you don't owe me shit, Midnight. I'm a big boy, I can take care of myself," Dallas said as he shut the door, his tone still carried the twinge of anger and frustration that was evident in the energy encompassing him, but there was also a hint of something else.

Remorse, perhaps.

But Midnight did not wish to think

about Dallas's startling fragile masculinity, and so she entered the bathroom, shutting the door just enough to give her privacy but cracking it just enough to vent the steam from her impending shower.

"Well, I wasn't about to let that attendant call the cops. We don't need that kind of trouble, or the attention. And besides, you're one of us now, and we take care of our own. Even if you don't appreciate it."

She turned the faucet on, testing the water until she found it to her liking.

"Of course, I appreciate it... fuck. Midnight..." Dallas huffed in annoyance.

"You keep saying I'm one of you, like the more you say it, the more it'll make it true." Dallas grunted. "But it's not true. I'm not one of you. I'm—"

"A hunter. Yes, you've made that quite clear. But you're also out of options, so just... Just accept it, and go to bed, okay? Don't argue with me." She sighed in exasperation.

The words came of their own accord, and once she'd said them, she realized how... *commanding* she sounded.

She'd never heard herself speak so... sternly to an adult. Midnight had always been polite, sweet even. Up until her untimely "death" at the tender age of twenty-five, she'd made every stride to keep the peace with people. She hated conflict. But she couldn't help but like the sound of her tone, or the way it made her feel.

Confidant, in charge.

The slight gasp from Dallas through the door caused butterflies in her stomach. His response was somehow fulfilling to her. She doubted a lot of people told Dallas *anything.* He didn't seem like the type to be told what to do.

Smirking in her own victory that she'd somehow rendered the sexy as sin hunter-Djinn speechless, she pulled out her phone, queuing up her favorite eighties playlist to listen to while she showered. The beginning synth of Eddie Money's *Take Me Home Tonight* filled the space as he sung about being hungry and exuding power.

She unbuttoned her jeans, sliding out of them with ease. The energy in the air shifted, and she could *sense* him just beyond the door. As if he was standing on the other side of it, waiting, keeping his distance.

The fact that a part of her *wanted*

him to throw open the door and stare at her with those vibrant, sapphire eyes of his, shirtless, looking all pissed off, should have been a red flag.

Actually, it should have been several red flags, but like that night eight years ago when a vampire touched her, she felt *compelled.*

Only this time, it was her who wanted to play.

To push Dallas.

Would he fall over the edge?

Or would he fight back?

Midnight removed her shirt, just as the door swung open, and a wicked grin pulled at the corners of her lips. She'd never felt so confidant and in control of any man before and the reality made her feel practically invincible.

She'd left the good girl she once was

back in the dirt when she'd died, when she'd lost everything and awakened someone else. Someone tougher, braver, hungrier, and in Dallas's presence... she was fearless.

Dallas stood there, shirtless, his double star tattoos standing out like headlights against his sweat-slicked golden skin, just below his perfectly taut nipples, pectorals glinting from the sweat in the light of the bathroom. The steam in the room clouded up, only adding to the inferno that existed in the canyon between them. He was only a mere feet away, but she longed to be closer.

Closer to his stormy scent, his heat.

Midnight knew she should scold him, tell him to get the hell out of her bathroom, and let her shower in peace.

To wait his turn.

It was the logical, practical thing to do.

But the blossoming heat between her legs was difficult to ignore, and she didn't want to do what she knew she *should* do. When Dallas entered her proximity, there were no rules, no boundaries. It was wild, dangerous, unexplored territory.

She wanted to blame the venom in her blood, the alcohol, or perhaps just an innate desire to be *owned* by enticing, sexy-as-hell monsters that made her feel alive and free. Whatever it was, she didn't want to fight what felt intrinsically *right*. Just like the night that changed her life.

Dallas took a step closer, his aura blood-red and rippling like a heatwave, distorting everything around him. The energy rolling off of him was thick like a fog, intense and somehow inciting. It called to her on a level she couldn't explain, so heavy it felt as if it had a life of its own.

Midnight stepped back in awe of its dark beauty, in awe of the vicious Viper that stood before her. She came up right against the cold, hard porcelain of the sink.

"You want to say that to my face, *Bambi,* hmm?" he said, his gaze and stance predatory. He looked at her like she was nothing more than a weak little fawn.

And in that one look, Midnight realized that he was baiting her, too.

She pushed off of the sink, feeling emblazoned by his gaze. He wanted to play, too, it seemed. She took a slow step toward him, now only inches away as she cocked her own head to the side, her gaze never leaving his neon eyes.

"Say what, *Viper*?" she whispered, her voice much darker than she'd ever heard it.

Dallas smirked, his tongue flicking out to trail over his lips as he shook his head slowly, arrogantly.

"You're playing with fire, Midnight. I'm warning you," he growled, closing the space between them. Steam surrounded them, turning the bathroom into some sort of lust-filled heaven.

Energy flared within her, ebbing like sunlight around her, around *them.*

And suddenly they were not Midnight and Dallas.

They were monsters.

Hungry, infected monsters.

"You don't call the shots *here*," she said as she licked her own lips, her fangs aching to *feed*.

It was as if the energy she'd consumed earlier was nothing more than an appetizer.

His skin was hot against hers as her bound breasts melded into him. Dallas's lips pulled back in a snarl, and she wasn't sure if he was going to *attack* her or kiss her.

She wasn't sure which she preferred, either.

Perhaps a little of both.

"Why won't you fucking let me be a good guy, for once?" he gritted out through his teeth. His gaze held her, stronger than any venom.

"Maybe I like broken things," she

whispered, feeling her own energy flare at the weight of their truth.

She'd never said such things out loud, and until this moment. The glass of her armor shattered around her as those words hung in the heated air between them. A deep growl rumbled from his chest as his jaw tensed, muscles rippling as his hands gripped the porcelain of the sink on both sides of her.

She was frozen in his gaze, staring up at him as his cock twitched against her, pulling her attention to his sizeable hardness for a moment. She fought the desire to look, to break his gaze, but she couldn't help herself.

A maddening blush formed in her cheeks from the moment of distraction, and Dallas struck like the viper he truly was. His movement was swift, brutal, as he grabbed her by the neck, his fingertips pressing on her jugular enough to show he was not playing around, but with enough give that she could easily break away.

At that moment, Midnight felt more alive than ever, welcoming the harsh touch all the same as she gazed up at him, her body speaking of its own accord.

He removed his hand from around her neck, leaving her skin feeling flush as he lifted her off the ground with ease, setting her on the edge of the counter with a thud as their lips crashed together.

It was a hazy, hot blur from there.

Midnight parted her lips instinctively, letting her tongue probe his, tasting his hunger, and the energy that flowed through him.

Mine.

She wasn't certain the thought in her brain belonged to her, but the word instilled a fire that was undeniable.

"Mine," Dallas growled, echoing the words in her consciousness like some sort of hex or curse. His tone was full of anger, of pain. But also there was a sliver of hope, as his wishful thoughts filled her consciousness.

The images that cycled through Midnight's brain were a flurry of love and pain, an endless tango to the death.

Jake Dallas had loved.

But he had also lost everything.

Yet, his wishful thoughts reverberated a sentiment Midnight understood with every fiber of her being.

He was *afraid.*

Afraid of losing all that mattered to him, afraid of starting over. Afraid to love again for fear it would only end in death.

Midnight ran her hands along his thick arms, squeezing his biceps with assurance, the word on her tongue foreign, but also cathartic.

"Yes," she said as she let her hands fall down his arms to his jeans, hurriedly unbuttoning them as energy filled her, making her entire body heat like a wildfire. She wasn't sure if she was answering his claim, his fear, or some deep-seated notion within herself that she was afraid to. Of falling over the edge into the unknown with someone she felt so strongly about since the moment she laid eyes on him in the Clam.

She barely knew Jake Dallas, but she

knew without a doubt that there was something monumental between them that couldn't be ignored. Sweat formed on her skin from the steam, the heat of his body, and the burgeoning desire to be ravaged by the beast before her.

To be slain by the *hunter* in her midst.

To come *home.*

Dallas grunted in her mouth as he rocked his hips forward with an involuntary thrust between her legs, which only served to add to her newfound hunger.

She wanted to devour him and all of his blood red, angry, frustrated, lustful energy.

His desire, his wishful thinking, was sweeter than anything she'd ever consumed before.

Consumed.

The realization that Dallas was *feeding* her was startling, but she couldn't focus on that.

She could only focus on sating the hunger in her heart, and the aching need to be filled, to be possessed until she found that blissful place again where she was everything and nothing all at once.

Dallas's lips grazed her jaw, the searing heat of his tongue over her throbbing pulse in her neck eliciting a desperate moan from her throat.

"We shouldn't fucking do this," he growled as he sucked at her sensitive flesh, his hands roving over her hips. His thumbs hooked into the sides of her panties, and he nearly *yanked* them off, rattling the entire sink and counter she was sitting on.

Flashbacks threatened to tear through with a vengeance, causing Midnight to grab onto his shoulders, wrapping her legs around him.

In her head she heard his turmoil, and it echoed her own.

He was right. They most certainly should not cross the line that had become so blurry in the matter of a night.

It's just the toxins in our blood, lowering our inhibitions, she told herself, but even she knew that wasn't entirely true. Her eyes fluttered shut as he peppered kisses over her jaw, her neck, her collarbone, his hands making quick work of unfastening her bra as she scooted herself closer to him, using her feet to kick his jeans and underwear to the floor in a pool around his ankles.

She needed to feel the friction, the heat of him against her. The hunger for all he could give her was maddening. She'd never felt quite this overwhelmed before, not even with Trevor.

It was both frightening and exciting all at once.

"I know," she whispered as she sank her nails into his shoulder, deep enough to pierce his skin.

Dallas groaned in her mouth, a sound so tortured it almost pulled her back from the ledge they teetered on. The room had become dense with steam as the shower rained against the naked tile floor, devoid of a subject to cleanse.

Dallas broke away for the sliver of a moment, gazing into her eyes, searching them for the one word that would make it all go away.

"Tell me to stop," he breathed, his entire body glowing with the intensity of wishful thinking as he set his large hands on the counter, boxing her in like the prey she was.

"Midnight... tell me to stop," he said, his voice catching in his throat as the unsaid words hung in the air between them with the pain rippling off of him.

Midnight bit her lip as his energy surrounded her, his scent, his wishful thinking too delicious to deny, and she had to admit she wanted all of it.

All of *him.*

The fire, the pain, the fear, the arrogance, the playfulness.

His broken, shattered heart that begged to be put together again, that begged to be cared for.

Midnight slid her hands up his neck, pulling him and his gaze to her own, finding a strength inside of her she hadn't known she possessed until he'd walked into her life.

It was that precise moment, Midnight knew she was doomed.

Because despite his prickly exterior, despite the fact she knew she absolutely shouldn't, she knew with the utmost certainty that she was falling for Dallas.

A tiny gasp escaped her throat as the reality hit her.

His blue eyes were full of hope, bright with the glow of a heartswish.

The most powerful wish there was next to a deathwish.

A wish that was more than a desire, or dream, and that was what she responded to.

ARIEL DAWN

"I don't want you to stop," she whispered as she tightened her legs around him, pulling him closer until they both dived off the cliffs into the uncharted waters below.

15

DALLAS STARED BACK at Midnight, torn between everything he knew he was and everything he wanted to be.

He wanted to blame his actions on his scratch fever. The impulsivity, the word vomit. His ankle itched to high hell, and his entire body felt like it was on fire, but it was like his inner walls had finally disintegrated. The walls he kept to protect himself, his heart from being broken.

He'd garnered that he kept his relationships without strings to protect himself from getting hurt. And he'd been content with that, even up until the point he wasn't, when he'd fallen for Ava.

But as Dallas looked in Midnight's eyes, as she ran her thumb along his jaw softly, bright blue eyes full of understanding and assurance, he realized that he'd never protected himself or his heart.

He'd only starved it.

And with that protective barrier diminished—in part to his fever—for the first time Dallas could just... be.

Alive, in the moment.

He didn't have to fight what felt right, what felt natural.

And Dallas couldn't deny that

Midnight's touch felt more than natural.

Memories flowed through his consciousness as she stared back at him.

Memories that did not belong to him, memories that enraged him.

Of Midnight being left alone, panic lacing through her.

Of tears that fell on familiar little blue lines, of doors slamming in her face and of running.

So much running.

The bombardment of loss, of pain, ebbed through him as he felt her memories like they were his own, and that was what he responded to. His protective instincts flared as he took her lips like a prayer, sliding his hands down her back, feeling her soft skin against his palms, relishing in the tiny shocks he got when he touched her.

Of a man who left her aching for a touch he never gave, a bliss he never shared with her except when it mattered only to him.

The sadness and desperation in her memories angered him. She'd given this man, this asshole, everything she was.

"Do you?" she whispered, her thumb brushing over his lips, her bright eyes looking as if she was on the verge of tears. Her voice shook slightly, sadness flaring the tornado building inside of him. He hated to see any woman cry, and more so hated to be the cause of it.

"Want to stop, I mean?" she asked, that same desperation, that same sadness in her tone as the one that filled his brain.

"No," Dallas said, the word heavy in

the air. He leaned his forehead against hers. The words were difficult as his demons threatened to escape through every fiber of his being.

"But I think..." He struggled with his own innate desire to give in not just to Midnight, but to himself as well.

He wanted nothing more than to drop to his knees and show her the appreciation she deserved. To drive her over the edge into oblivion, over and over, to see if she tasted as good as she smelled.

Because she smelled like sex on a fucking stick.

"I think *you* deserve more, Midnight," he said with heavy breath.

"That's not my name," she whispered, leaning her forehead against his.

"What?" His breath caught in his

throat.

"Midnight isn't my name. It's Faith." Her voice shook as she said the words, and in that moment, Dallas's heart swelled, his entire being understanding that Midnight had given him more than just her name.

It was more than permission, more than assurance.

It was a wish.

Would he grant it?

Was he capable of doing so?

Did he want to?

"Faith." Her name on his tongue was like an unanswered prayer, the answer to all of life's mysteries.

Faith.

That was what he needed, but Dallas wasn't ready to believe he could have such things. Even if he wanted them.

"Come on, let's... let's get you cleaned up before they kick us out of this joint for running up the water bill," he said, his voice shaking. His cock ached, the desire for release maddening, but Dallas wanted more.

More than a fever, alcohol-induced, guilty romp with a woman who made him feel alive again.

Midnight nodded slowly in understanding.

"O... okay," she said, sadness lacing her words.

The feeling of rejection flourished in him and his consciousness from their *bond*. Because he knew with certainty, what existed between them was something deeper than just the fact they were both monsters.

His grip tightened on her as he held

her close, pulling her off of the counter, clutching her body to him with a force that was both familiar and somehow new. She tightened her arms around his neck, wetness blooming against his skin as she held onto him. He carried her to the running shower, running his hand up and down her back as he angled them both under the shower. It was a tight fit, with his size, and he was half out of the spray, but he didn't care.

Midnight's legs slid down his sides, and he could feel her energy wavering. She was tired, and so was he. She turned around, pleading blue eyes calling to him with sadness and guilt that echoed in the space between them.

"I'm sorry," she said, her shoulders slumping.

"I—"

Dallas ran his hands over her head, sliding his fingers down her silky black hair, his gaze holding her still.

"Don't do that. Don't apologize to me because you think you did something wrong. Because you think I don't want you."

Midnight turned her head away, but Dallas gently guided it back, cocking his head to the side to capture her gaze.

"Jake..."

"Because I do. Want you." The words fell out of his mouth, like he was possessed. And in a way, perhaps he was.

Possessed by hope, by wolf venom, alcohol, and the unfathomable, undeniable truth.

He'd played the same game for so long, used to the same results it yielded.

But not this time.

This time, Dallas wanted a different outcome. A better one.

A Happy Ever After, if there was one for him.

Looking in Midnight—no, Faith's glassy blue eyes, he dared to wish there was.

"Please don't cry." His deep voice fell, his knees feeling weak. Instinct swelled within him as he slid his hand up her neck resting his palm on her jaw. The need to brush away all the tears and pain was damn near overwhelming, and it scared Dallas far more than any monster.

How can I fall so fast for a woman I barely know...

A knock on the door pulled Dallas from his dangerous thoughts and made them both jump.

"Fuck," Dallas said, his lips pursed together as he looked away.

"It's probably your stuff," Midnight said as she turned away from him, the water raining down her back, her slick, silky black hair making her pale skin all the brighter. Dallas's heart *ached.*

I fucked up. Shit.

"Faith..."

"Just go. It's fine. I'll finish up here on my own. I'm a big girl. I can take care of myself."

Dallas felt conflicted. He didn't *want* to leave her alone. In fact, he wanted to do the opposite. He wanted to wrap his arms around Midnight and protect her from the ghosts that haunted her, wanted to dispel all the pain and trauma so that she'd never hurt again. But he knew the concierge would keep knocking...

He stepped out of the shower reluctantly, grabbing a towel. He longed to say something, anything to kill the thick tension in the air, his cock still throbbing with the hope of finding release, and he adjusted himself if only to quiet the desire and avoid an awkward moment. It wasn't like she could see him anyway with her back to him.

He grabbed his underwear and jeans, the memory of the wildfire of moments ago still fresh in his brain and cock.

How Midnight had wrapped her legs around him, pulling him closer to her heated core.

How he'd almost given in.

It had taken him far too much

concentration to stay in control.

In the presence of Midnight, Dallas felt out of control.

And he hated to feel out of control.

Because I don't call the shots, here.

As he walked out of the bathroom toward the ominous door in nothing but his underwear, he looked over his shoulder at the bathroom door, letting the guilt rack him.

But he was used to guilt.

It was an age-old friend.

Dallas opened the door, not giving any shits about the scrawny concierge who had brought him back to reality. To his surprise, there was no one standing in the darkness. The cot leaned against the side of the door, his backpack in front of it.

He took the folded up cot and

backpack, slowly making his way back inside. Closing the door, he tossed his backpack on the ground as he set the cot up on the opposite side of Midnight's bed, closest to the door.

When he turned around, Midnight stood in the bathroom doorway, a white towel wrapped around her. Their eyes met for a moment. Just before he spoke, she did.

"Rebel sent a text. Apparently the wolves have agreed to help us. There will be a meeting at sunset tomorrow in The Badlands to go over plans for the carnival."

"Carnival?" Dallas asked as he stood up straighter.

Midnight fingered through her duffel bag at the edge of her bed, pulling out a fresh pair of underwear and black pajama pants with pink bunnies on them. The sight made Dallas crack a small smile.

The woman he'd come to know was somewhat of an enigma to him. An amalgamation of things that were all so different, but enmeshed to create a being of complexity and beauty.

Midnight was like a *ying-yang*. Equal parts soft and hard, dark and light.

Monstrous and human.

And she was quite beautiful, though Dallas knew the Djinn DNA had likely finessed her much in the way vampire DNA made its parasites more pleasing, but he would have bet his last dollar that she was just as stunning before the Djinn DNA took over.

"Yeah, Amora said the wolves agreed to bump up their yearly carnival in favor of trying to trap the vamps. The Boracellis got some of their own in there," she said softly as she dropped the towel.

Dallas wanted to look away, because he knew it was the polite, right thing to do. But he couldn't help himself.

Like a moth to a flame, resistance was futile.

Her beauty kept him in place like Medusa, causing his stone-hard cock to twitch with anticipation.

In the low light of the room, her pale skin stood out like moonlight. Her nipples were still pert, and Dallas told himself it was from the onslaught of the chill of the air, that it had nothing to do with what had happened between them—what *almost* happened—and it most certainly had nothing to do with the way he was looking at her.

Her wet hair fell around her shoulders, and his gaze traveled to her abdomen, the sight of the small patch of darkness just below her navel flaring his inner demons, begging them to surface again.

He took a deep breath as he adjusted himself, turning around, closing his eyes as he braced himself against his cot.

"Great," he grunted.

"Okay, well, I'm beat. I'll see you in the afternoon," she said, her voice full of hope, tinged with exhaustion.

Dallas nodded.

"Yeah. See you in the afternoon."

***

Thunder cracked, so loud the room shook.

Dallas groaned as he tossed and turned on his cot, trying to find a comfortable spot, but it was no use. The rain poured outside as the wind howled, and he half wondered if the damn motel would go up in a twister and spit him out in a universe where he wasn't the bad guy.

Because that was how he felt.

Like a perpetual villain.

Always coming up short, always letting everyone down. Aside from tracking down the vampires who'd killed his wife and putting a stake through their hearts—which had not provided him the peace he thought it would.

He was a formidable hunter. He knew his stakes and blades well, and he could exorcise demons just as good as any demonologist, but when it came to matters of the heart, he told himself he was happy being the bad guy.

If it protected the ones he loved, he could stomach the disdain, the anger, and even the rejection.

At least, that was what he told himself, but now... he was not so sure.

The sound of a gut-wrenching cry startled him without warning, and he jumped up immediately, upending the damn contraption he was supposed to sleep on.

Instinct kicked in, the flight or fight mode he'd been living for the last sixteen years his autopilot. He reached for his backpack, grabbing the knife he had stashed from the Clam as another round of thunder cracked. The darkness of the room only added to the fright as Dallas searched the shadows for the intruder.

"No, stop!" the voice cried out, all desperation and terror. Lightning lit up the room in a flash of white, and Dallas could see there was no intruder.

But there was a writhing woman in the throws of a viscous nightmare on the queen bed mere feet away.

Dallas dropped his knife without thinking. He approached Midnight with the same haste he would have a monster, if one had actually shown up. He stood at the side of her bed, watching as her hands reached out for the sheets, grasping at them as his own memories trapped him.

"Ahhhh! Dallas... something's wrong!" Ava cried, clutching her neck.

"Stay with it, Ava... We're almost there..." he coaxed her, the incubus demon buried inside of the renowned

demonologist Ava had been fucking was nearly home free, to be trapped forever in a crystal.

To hear Ava cry was like a shockwave to his entire system. Ava Crowley did not cry for anything. Like him, her heart was made of stone.

The blood on her neck pulled his attention as he realized what had happened.

She'd been bitten.

The incubus had already started his mating ritual, and if she didn't get an antidote soon...

And then Cassius showed up.

Dallas scrambled to get up, after being knocked down from the blast of the crystal. His ears rang, his vision blurred.

Cassius crawled closer to Ava, and he hollered, but she could not hear him.

His body ached from the impact, and he struggled to stand. He needed to get to her...

"Cas!" she called out, her voice edged in pain and terror. "Make it stop..."

Dallas felt the impact of her words like someone had struck a dagger in his *heart and set him on fire.*

It is just the bond, nothing more. She doesn't... she can't... she's not thinking straight, he thought.

"I'm here," Cassius purred, his hand resting on the blood of her neck.

Lightning flashed again, pulling Dallas from his haunted memories.

Memories that still hurt.

But the sight of Midnight's face, twisted in agony as she cried out, "No, take me instead, please..." reminded him that there was nothing he could do about the past.

But he could do something about the present.

Dallas leaned on the edge of the bed, reaching a shaky hand out to Midnight. He set his palm on her shoulder, shaking her lightly.

"Midnight, wake up." His voice shook as the memories continued to try and pull him back under.

He crawled up on top of the bed as another clash of thunder rang, shaking Midnight. She twisted and turned, fingers grabbing at the bedsheets, making contact with his thigh. Her nails sunk deep into his flesh, but the sting was minimal compared to the pain he could feel all throughout his body.

"Laura!" Dallas cried out as he ran through the crime scene tape.

"Mr. Dallas..." the officer called out to him, but he didn't care.

"Let him go, Detective. He's just a kid. She's not going to make it to the hospital..."

His eyes fell on her, tied to the gurney, blood permeating her pink dress.

Terror ran through him. Remorse swelled like a hurricane as he told himself he should have been there.

He should have protected her...

"Jake..." she whispered, her voice weak.

"I'm here, baby, I'm here..." he said, tears threatening to fall like a waterfall. He rested his hand over hers, which was gently clutching her belly.

"I'm sorry..." she whispered.

"Baby, there's nothing to be sorry about, just... stay with me, okay."

Laura's head rolled to the side as she closed her eyes, letting out a sigh of contentment. He could see what looked like bite marks on her slender neck, on her wrists and thighs, where her bloodied dress was bunched up. He covered her with his body.

"I'm cold," she whispered, and Dallas felt her touch like ice.

Instinctively, he pulled off his flannel, doing his best to wrap her in his warmth and keep her decent. If he could just keep her warm enough...

"I'll keep you warm, baby. I promise, just keep talking to me..."

"I love you," she murmured as her hand fell.

"I know, baby, I love you, too. Just... stay with me, okay?" he said, tears prickling the edges of his eyes. He was

terrified, as the world around him spun out of control.

"I think Kelly and I just need some sleep..."

"No, Laura, listen to me. Don't..."

He reached for her hand, but she did not grab on.

"Wake up, Laura, come on..." he cried. His entire body shook as he shook her.

She felt lifeless.

"Midnight..." he called again, his voice stronger, now.

"Wake up, come on..."

The anger and sadness that filled him also fueled him.

He would not give in to the darkness again, he would not let the blood of the lost destroy everything he'd done since, he would not let it destroy the man he'd built from its ashes.

"Faith, wake up!" he yelled, and she sat up with a scream. Her fingernails squeezed his leg as her right hand clutched her shirt to her chest.

"Emma!" she cried as sobs wracked her body.

Without thinking, as relief flooded him, Dallas pulled Midnight close, wrapping his arms around her. She was bathed in cold sweat.

"It's okay, you're okay. It was just a..."

Midnight wrapped her arms around Dallas's tree trunk of a waist, and the relief where she'd sunk her nails into his skin was faint. He scrambled to pull her between his legs, wrapping her in a scratch-fever fueled cocoon of warmth as he held onto her tight. He set his chin on top of her silky, black hair, and for the first time since he'd lost his wife, he cried.

Because the pain radiating through him wasn't just his pain, no.

He knew what it was like to lose those you loved.

He knew what it was like to have everything taken away from you.

And in the darkness of that shared pain, as the wind whipped and the rain slammed against the motel, Dallas finally let go.

16

THE WORLD MOVED in slow motion around Midnight as Dallas pulled her into his arms, against his warm chest. The sparks that usually shocked her every time she touched him had gone from tiny little jolts to a full blown powder keg as her entire body lit up from the inside out.

No man or monster had ever *held* her like this. Like she was worth protecting, like she was safe. Like somehow everything was going to be okay, despite the last four years being full of dead-ends.

The rumble in Dallas's chest echoed her own as his memories filled her brain.

Memories of a beautiful blonde-haired woman in a white maxi dress with a tiny bouquet of carnations under a gazebo, of the same woman curled up on the couch beside him, with a noticeable baby bump, bathed in the light of the television, eating popcorn from a gigantic bowl. Of painting the nursery pink. Of laughter, and love.

So much love.

Of her eyes fluttering shut, her hand falling from underneath his.

The sadness, the pain, and the immense guilt flooded through her like a tidal wave as she ran her hands up his warm skin, along his muscles in his back.

"What was her name?" she whispered.

Dallas's chest rumbled as his body shook.

"Laura."

Midnight pulled away for only a fraction as she looked up at him. Her own energy reached for him, tangling with his pain, soothing it.

"She was beautiful," Midnight said as she reached up to wipe a stray tear making its way down his cheek.

And to her surprise, he let her.

Dallas did not fight or grumble, nor did he push her away. Instead, he only gazed down at her with a sense of understanding, his eyes speaking words his tongue could not.

He pursed his lips, closing his eyes as he nodded slowly.

"She was... she was my everything," he said, opening his eyes once more, gazing down at Midnight. "They tell you it gets easier, but... it doesn't, does it?"

Midnight shook her head.

"No, it doesn't. You just get better at hiding it."

Dallas pulled her closer.

"You were screaming..." His voice softened.

"I panicked."

"It felt so real," she said as she leaned into him with ease, running her hands through his hair in a soothing, caring motion.

It had felt real. It felt real every time the nightmare reared its ugly head, reminding her of all that she had lost. What she was truly fighting for.

In the darkness, amidst the storm raging outside, Midnight felt the world shift inside of her.

She felt a *bond* with Jake Dallas that she had never quite experienced with anyone else.

A bond she *wished* she could have had with Emma's father.

"I know," he murmured as his gaze fell to her lips.

"But it's not real. You're here, you're alive, and you'll get her back," he said, his voice full of wishful thinking and unbreakable promises.

Midnight wanted to believe him. She wanted to have faith.

His hands traveled along her back as she shifted in between his legs, kneeling in between them to meet his height. Upright he towered over her, nearly six feet tall to her petite, five foot something. Rain pitter-pattered against the window like claws scratching, like demons threatening to take her under.

"I promise," he whispered.

The words were more powerful than any wishful thinking.

Because they were more than just words to a Djinn.

Dallas's promise was a *heartswish.*

And the reality of what that meant caused Midnight's aura to burn brighter than any star, caused her heart to swell.

Midnight crushed her lips to his without a second thought, filling him with the vibrant wonder of love and understanding that was truly the foundation of a heartswish.

She poured every ounce of herself into him, and Dallas did not relent. He kissed her back with the fire of a thousand suns, like the dam had broken, his fingers sliding just beneath the waistband of her pajama pants, hovering just above the flesh of her ass.

His energy vibrated around them, dancing with hers as he pulled her closer, leaning back against the headboard.

Midnight followed his lead as he settled against the bed, leaning into his frame. His rigid hardness pressed against her thighs, causing her pulse to race, her breath to catch in her throat. Instinctively, she let her hands slide down his chest, past his abdomen until she found his sizeable thickness. Hunger flared in the bond between them, desire filling their shared conscious space.

She squeezed him through the warm, moist fabric of his boxers, and Dallas grunted in response.

"Tell me to stop," she purred, feeling emblazoned in the heat that surrounded them. The undeniable ache to be filled returned, but it was insurmountable, absolutely nothing to the *need* to be bound to this man, this monster.

Her *mate*.

Dallas slid his hand underneath her pajama pants around to just below her navel. He slid his fingers through her coarse hair, rubbing little massaging circles over her sensitive mound.

"I don't want you to fucking stop, Midnight." His voice was full of desire, of wishful thinking.

But it was the mutual love in their

bond that radiated clearer than any desire or wish. It was raw, deep, and honest.

Her own words came out of their own volition as she released his cock, a frustrated groan leaving his mouth. The heat of Dallas's gaze could be felt like an entity of its own, and she watched briefly as he grabbed himself with his free hand through his boxers, while watching her intently.

"I didn't say you could do that," she said, a newfound energy filling her. The energy in the room shifted as Midnight removed her shirt, her nipples hardening as the cool air kissed her skin.

She removed her pajama pants before sliding between Dallas's legs like a snake, brushing her bare breasts along his chest as she gently pulled his hand away. She wasn't certain how she knew what he needed, other than it was pure magic. Magic fed to her through a bond she'd never thought she'd discover, but one she was happy to have discovered all the same.

Her insides ached, her heart raced.

For *him.*

Her mate.

Dallas's lips curved into a sexy smile as he hooked his fingers into the side of her panties, tugging the straps roughly.

"So fucking bossy," he growled.

Midnight smiled in return as she slid her hands in between his boxer's waistband, sliding them down as best she could from the close proximity.

But Dallas seemed to have other plans as he lunged forward, unpending Midnight onto her back with a soft thud into the mattress, grasping her by the thighs. He deftly removed her panties over her ankles, tossing them aside with ease. He leaned closer, the head of his cock just inches away from her entrance.

Midnight whimpered in defeat.

"Is this what you want?" he said, his voice full of lust, heavy with command as he shimmied out of his boxers completely.

Midnight felt as if she couldn't breathe. Everything around her converged into him, into the bond between them that was stronger than the storm raging outside.

"Yes," she moaned in response, the word heavy with the weight of the truth.

His tone shifted to a cocky one. In the grey haze of the light pouring in from the storm, he looked every bit a vicious, dangerous snake.

But Midnight couldn't deny that perhaps she wanted his bite more than she knew.

"What do you say?"

"Please," Midnight groaned, not missing a beat. His energy fed her, filled her up like an overflowing teacup.

Dallas slid a finger through her sensitive folds and Midnight could not help but reflexively tilt her hips, seeking more of the friction. It had been far too long since she'd felt anyone's touch but her own, and it was too hard to keep quiet. Not now, not that her insides were swirling, her desire cycling like a whirlpool.

He settled her legs around his neck, building a steady rhythm with his fingers. A torturous rhythm.

"Please, what?" he taunted her as he lifted her from her ass with his free hand, bringing his lips down to her slick center, taking her clit into his mouth and sucking while he slid another finger in.

Her insides clutched him, as her orgasm started to pool like a sweltering cyclone. Around and around it went, as she bucked her hips, wishing for more. More of his tongue, his fingers, his touch.

She couldn't remember any of her former lovers ever making her feel quite like *this*.

In fact, Midnight was certain none of them had ever brought her so close to the edge as she was right now, just from their tongue alone. The revelation was equal parts wonderful and frightening. It would be over soon, and she didn't want such things to end.

"Please, Dallas, I'm going to..." Midnight's eyes shut as her orgasm hit her out of nowhere, her vision going white.

She tightened her legs around his neck, holding on for dear life as it tore through her. She expected him to drop her, now that she'd finished, certainly she'd need to tend to him...

But Dallas did no such thing.

In fact, he only grabbed her thighs with so much force she was certain he'd leave a mark, removing his fingers altogether as he continue to suck, sliding his tongue inside of her pulsating walls.

"Oh, fucking hell," she said as her

body rode the wave of the most intense orgasm she'd ever felt. She felt like a live wire dancing in a puddle.

I'm not done with you yet, Bambi. Not by a long shot.

His voice in her brain was not startling, only relieving.

Please, I need—

Dallas dropped her legs, and they fell to the mattress with a thud. She looked up at him, his aura the brightest white she'd ever seen. His blue eyes glowed aquamarine, and the reflection glinted off his wet lips and chin, causing her insides to cyclone again. In the light, his aura, his tan skin took on an angelic golden hue.

Midnight took in the sight of him, all hard lines and edges, tattoos, and shadows. Her gaze fell to where he stroked his thick, swollen cock, and her heart raced. Blood rushed into her cheeks as she realized how small Trevor had been in comparison.

"I know what you... fuck!" Dallas cursed as Midnight lunged forward of her own accord, knocking him back into the sheets with much heavier thud.

Thanks to being a Djinn, Midnight possessed a strength she hadn't when she was mortal, not that she liked to use it much.

In fact, she preferred not to use it outside of battles like the one they'd engaged in prior, and was startled at the amount of strength she'd used to push Dallas down, as if some other entity had taken over.

The desire to possess this man, this Djinn, her mate... was overwhelming.

The bond ebbed between them, and Midnight knew exactly what it wanted.

It needed to lay root once and for all, and entwine itself into a *solidified*, impenetrable bond.

One that nothing could break.

Midnight held Dallas in place with her hands on his chest, angling her body over his. She brought her lips to his, kissing him adamantly, the taste of herself on his lips and tongue sweeter than she'd thought it would be.

Dallas groaned in her mouth as his tongue slid over hers, his hands settling at her bare ass as he pushed her down, brushing his hardness against her still sensitive mound.

Midnight giggled in his mouth as she shook her head.

"I told you, you don't call the shots

here, Jake."

Dallas bit at her lip as she let out another giggle.

"You are fucking relentless, I'll give you that," he purred, traipsing his mouth over her collarbone, down to her breast, taking her taut nipple in his teeth.

The pain of his bite felt... good.

She wanted to feel his fangs pierce her skin.

It was a sweet kind of pain Midnight had never known, but wanted more of.

She wanted more of this man who made her head spin, who called to her heart and promised her the world.

Who would shield her from the storms that threatened her, in so many ways, if she let him.

And she would do the same.

"Is this what you want?" she purred, taunting him as she ground her hips against him, teasing him.

Dallas let out another curse as his entire body tensed, as his fingers gripped her hips, digging into her skin.

"Yes," he grunted, his tone full of sweet venom.

Midnight gazed down at him, his aura bright like a halo, eyes glowing with need. She watched them fall shut in ecstasy, in relief as she slid herself over his thickness, relishing in the stretch as their bodies came together like fire and ice.

"Fuck," Dallas groaned, his head falling back against the headboard, his voice full of emotion that Midnight could feel all throughout her body.

The moment of stillness seemed like

an eternity until he'd bottomed out. His hands slid over her flesh. With his right hand he guided her hips, his left hand finding her breast to tease her nipple. When he looked at her, she could see the universe in his eyes, and she knew, nothing would ever be the same again.

"Mine," she said, her voice clear as a bell.

Dallas rocked his hips, thrusting into her with solid force as her orgasm started to culminate again. He built a slow, deep rhythm, the sound of the storm outside a symphony of the passion brewing between them.

Round and round it went, the beat of their hearts and heavy breathing like angels singing.

Dallas slid his hand over her breast, up her neck and into her hair. He held her gaze with a strength she could feel like a ghost, covering her, blanketing her like armor.

He nodded hazily, his thrusts becoming erratic as he chased his release in tandem with her.

"Yes," he murmured, his breath heavy with the power of truth and promise.

"And you're mine," he said as he sat up, causing his cock to hit places Midnight had never even known existed.

As his lips moved against hers, she fell into the darkness, into the intoxicating scent and warm hold of her mate as his thrusts came to a halt, as the crescendo of her orgasm culminated.

Dallas broke away from her lips, burying his head into her shoulder, his arms encasing her as if he never wanted to let her go.

"Yes," Midnight answered, her truth resonating in the space between them. His cock throbbed inside of her as he emptied himself, his heartbeat synchronizing with hers.

He pulled her back with him as he lay down, still buried to the hilt within her. Exhaustion hit them both, evident in their bond as the rain started to let up.

It felt as if she was both invigorated, but also depleted at the same time.

Slumber seemed like a good idea.

The feel of him vacating her caused a strange sort of sadness to swell. She didn't want him to leave...

The memories of her past threatened to darken the bliss she felt, and her heart caught in her throat.

Don't go... she said inside their

shared consciousness, panic and fear taking over as the remains of their tryst dampened the inside of her thighs.

Dallas curled himself around her frame, pulling her closer to his chest as he once again buried his face in her hair.

"I'm not going anywhere," he murmured sleepily.

"Promise?" she asked, feeling the familiar anxieties telling her he wasn't any different than Trevor. That he wasn't any different than any of the assholes she'd fallen for in the past.

Dallas held her with a warm, solid grip as he whispered in her ear sleepily, "I promise."

17

DALLAS AWOKE FEELING better than
he'd felt in a long time. Especially since
he'd awakened as a hungry monster.

The sun shone through the motel
window, bathing Midnight in its golden
glow like some sort of angel.

Midnight was flush against his chest,
her silky black hair tickling his nipples,
and reality hit him like he'd wiped out
on his motorcycle.

We fucked.

No, Dallas knew it was much more than just a rogue fuck.

Because when he looked at Midnight, sound asleep in his arms, little soft snores escaping her parted lips, he knew there was nothing he wouldn't do for her, despite knowing logically he'd only known her for barely a week.

We bonded.

The word filled his brain, and somehow he understood that it was the right word for what had happened. Dallas had been no stranger to anonymous, casual sex in the years since he'd become a full fledged hunter, and he'd even fallen in love again and had *connected* sex.

But nothing felt as good, as right, as the memory of being inside of Midnight.

Because for once, Dallas felt *complete.* Like he'd found the missing piece of a puzzle he hadn't known he was looking for.

It didn't make sense to him, because he thought he'd found his missing piece nearly sixteen years ago, but Dallas was starting to understand that not everything needed an explanation. That some things are more than what they appeared to be, if he only looked a little harder.

That not all Djinn were bloodthirsty harlots out to kill humans.

That not all vampires were selfish bloodthirsty ticks.

And that a broken road could still lead to beautiful places.

Instinctively, Dallas pulled Midnight closer, letting his fingers slide through her soft hair, letting himself *feel* her for the first time.

In the still of the afternoon sunlight, his heart beat steadily, his leg did not itch, his body temperature felt... normal, and he felt at *peace*.

I never thought I'd see peace again, not like this... I almost feel... human.

Midnight stirred, her dark lashes fluttering against her skin.

"You're still here," she murmured, almost surprised.

Of course I'm here... he thought, not even caring if she heard his thoughts.

"I told you I wasn't going anywhere," he said calmly.

The relief that flashed over her expression made his heart swell and he was powerless against the bright sparkle in her eye. So he leaned in and kissed her softly as she entwined her fingers in his hair.

"How's your leg?" she asked as she broke away from his lips, sliding her leg between his. His cock twitched with anticipation.

"My bite? I don't feel anything, actually... I think... I think it's healed."

Midnight smiled, and the sight was a balm to his damn soul.

Dallas felt energized, confident in a way he hadn't in ages.

"How are you feeling?" he asked, his voice dropping an octave as his gaze fell to her lips.

A part of him was nervous, though he couldn't explain why. But panic flooded him all the same. Perhaps it was a history of leaving in the morning to avoid attachment. To avoid being hurt.

"Amazing, actually. But also... um... I think I need a shower."

Dallas couldn't help the laugh that erupted out of his chest, and Midnight giggled herself.

"Fair enough," he said, a smile cracking his face for the first time in ages.

"However... should you need some help..." he teased as he pulled her closer, planting soft kisses along her lips, jaw, neck, biting at the sensitive flesh with his teeth, causing her to let out a sweet laugh of her own.

"Hmmm, tempting..." she replied wickedly, neither of them aware of the mechanical clicking of a card being registered.

When the door swung open, they both turned in shock, to see a red-faced Boo and Rebel rolling her eyes.

"Pay up," Rebel deadpanned as she looked at Boo.

"For fuck's sake..." Boo said as he dug in his pocket for a stack of bills.

Midnight clutched the sheets to herself, but Dallas had never cared about preserving himself.

It certainly wasn't the first time someone had stumbled in on him after the fact.

"You ever fucking heard of knocking?" he bit.

Rebel rolled her eyes.

"We have bigger shit to worry about than where you two are playing hide the dipstick," Rebel touted as she popped a hand on her hip.

Dallas lazily got up, giving both Boo and Rebel an ample show as he picked his clothes up off the floor.

Midnight held the sheets to her chest, biting her lip as a blush stained her perfectly pale cheeks.

Immediately the thought of turning other cheeks pink coursed through his brain, and he did not push it away.

Midnight turned to him with wide eyes, and he only smirked.

He no longer cared if she could hear his thoughts.

In fact, he *wanted* her to know how he really felt, the things that went through his mind... because it felt *good* to share, to be understood.

To be connected with her, to her...

"What's that?" Midnight said as he stepped into his boxers.

"Amora and the Mayfields are getting shit up and running today for this carnival they think is going to draw the vamps out like moths to a flame," Rebel said.

Dallas slid into his jeans.

Midnight stayed in bed behind her sheets.

"And what does that have to do with *us* exactly?" Dallas griped.

"It's likely to draw a big crowd. We'll be set up to patrol in groups," Boo said, looking everywhere but at him or Midnight.

Dallas rolled his eyes.

"Wouldn't it make sense to patrol or put forces on the property when they *aren't* there? Ambush those bloodsuckers when they get back?" he asked.

Rebel shrugged.

"We don't make the calls. Amora

does. You got a problem with it, take it up with her."

Dallas gritted his teeth. He'd promised Midnight they'd find a way to get her daughter back, and he meant it. But it seemed like Sweet Valley Vamp and the wolf pack were completely missing a solid chance to get the vamps unattended.

"Not to mention, how do we *know* the vamps are going to show up to the carnival?" Dallas asked, not bothering to throw on a shirt.

Rebel scoffed.

"It's a group of humans in one *confined* space. It's like shooting fish in a fucking barrel."

"You think the vamps are that stupid?" Dallas asked.

Boo and Rebel looked at him in

confusion.

"Amora knows how to pull the vamps. She's one of them, remember? Or did you hit your head on the headboard a little too hard when you decided to rail my fucking friend last night?" Rebel bit.

Dallas's temper flared.

"Since you're a *friend,* I'm going to choose to let your bitch ass comment go. This isn't some fucking monster reality show. However, I know vamps better than you probably do. I've been killing them for sixteen fucking years." The air in the room became incredibly thick with his words. Dallas squared his shoulders as he spoke.

"You don't just dangle blood in front of vamps, but I'm sure you know that given the face that you all seduced a bunch of idiots into the Marquis for vamp chow." Dallas turned as he realized his words, looking at Midnight, whose eyes looked hurt, and he instantly hated himself.

Her thoughts filled him with sadness. *I did what I had to do to survive.*

Dallas's shoulders loosened, his eyebrows furrowing.

I'm sorry, I didn't mean...

Midnight wrapped the sheets around her as she got out of the bed.

"Midnight, I—"

"It's fine, *Viper.* I'm getting a shower." Her tone was tired, if a bit icy. She left him standing there with Boo and Rebel, who looked at him with disapproval.

"I just meant..."

"We know what you meant. But you know, just because we've done shit, doesn't mean we liked it. We do what we have to do to survive, Viper. Not all of us can feed on energy without getting our fangs dirty. Amora provides for us, so we don't question the hand that feeds us. And you shouldn't either," Rebel said as she turned around.

Boo sighed.

"Give us a minute, Reby," he said sternly.

Rebel threw her hands up.

"You're wasting your time, but whatever," she said as she left.

It was only Boo and Dallas. Before he could speak, Boo stepped closer.

"The wolves have their parts to play, too. We been given orders to not attack publicly, 'cus civilians and all... but there's a fun house. It's dark, only a few folks go in at a time..." Boo said calmly, his gaze meeting Dallas's.

The candor of his tone, his shrug, and his demeanor told Dallas all he needed to know. The sound of the shower turned on behind them.

"Accidents happen." Boo shrugged.

"Just thought you should know," he said, glancing at the bathroom door.

Dallas nodded in response.

"And just know, I ain't above killing, either, *Viper*. Especially if someone's a threat to my family."

Dallas stood still as Boo flashed his long, white fangs. The energy rolling off of him was deadly serious, and Dallas respected him more because of it. It was clear the man cared for Midnight, and Rebel, perhaps saw them as daughters even. Dallas met his gaze, nodding.

"I understand," he said solidly.

Boo nodded in response.

"Good. 'Cuz, I like ya. I really don't want to hafta to kill ya."

Dallas sighed.

"That makes two of us."

Boo turned to leave, stopping just in front of the door.

"We have a meeting at The Badlands in an hour," he said as he left, shutting the door quietly.

Dallas turned around, staring at the bathroom door. He felt afraid in an entirely new way. He'd fought monsters nearly his entire adult life, but nothing scared him as much as the wrath, or the rejection he might walk into. Which he well deserved. He'd been an ass. But the soft ebbing pull in his heart told him apologizing was the right thing to do, and so that was what he followed.

He stopped just in front of the shower

curtain, taking in the sight of Midnight's silhouette.

"I'm sorry," he said softly.

"What?" Midnight said.

"I can't hear you over the water..." she said.

Dallas stepped closer, pulling the curtain aside just enough to speak louder.

"I said I'm sorry," he tried again. Guilt, shame, and anger wracked him.

Midnight pulled the shower curtain open, standing in front of him, naked, wet, and...

"I'm sorry for being an asshole, I just..." He huffed. He grabbed her towel, handing it to her as a peace offering.

"I'm not good at this normally, and I've never been with a..."

"A what?" Midnight asked as she

grabbed the towel, her bright gaze never leaving his.

Dallas wanted to say the word *monster*, because he knew that was what she was. But he was a monster, too, and somehow that just didn't sound right. It didn't feel right.

"I've never been with someone of the fanged variety," he said dryly.

Midnight laughed. She laughed a sarcastic, annoyed laugh.

"You mean you've never been with a *monster* you've killed," she said honestly. The words fell on Dallas, heavy on his shoulders.

It hurt to hear them, but she was right.

"You're not a monster, Midnight," he said, his voice dropping along with his gaze.

She tied the towel around herself, stepping up to him. Which was a feat, given she was nearly a foot smaller than him.

"And neither are you, Jake," she said with a sigh.

"I know what you are. I knew the day I met you in the Clam. I knew you could kill me then, but you didn't." Her voice fell.

"I didn't want to kill you," he said softly.

"Why not?" she asked as she lifted his chin.

He looked down at her, long wet hair splayed over her shoulders. Dallas had to think about her question. He'd never really thought about why he'd let her go, telling himself it was because he was distracted by Ava and Cassius... But perhaps he'd let her go because on some level he knew Midnight was not a killer.

She was *good.*

"Because you're different," he said.

Midnight let her fingers travel through the edges of his hair. He was acutely aware of the barriers between them, both physical and mental.

"Do you know why I rescued you?" she asked quietly.

Dallas shook his head.

"Because I'm pretty?" he quipped, gesturing to himself cockily, his tone dry and witty if only because the seriousness of her tone, of the energy between them, was making him nervous. He couldn't remember feeling this nervous since he'd decided to ask Laura to marry him.

Midnight shook her head.

"Because that night I met you in the

Clam, I knew you were different, too. You could have killed me. But you didn't. You could have killed me that night at the Marquis, when I found you. You could have killed me anytime in the last seven days, but you didn't. Because you, too, did what you had to do to *survive*."

Dallas sighed in defeat, closing his eyes.

"But who we *were*, Jake... it's not who we *are* now, is it?" she asked softly.

Dallas shook his head.

"No, it's not," he said, opening his eyes to stare into sapphire pools of understanding.

"So I can't judge you on what you did. I can only judge you on what you do now, understand?" she whispered.

Dallas nodded.

"Yeah, I understand," he said.

"Good. Because the next time you talk out of your ass like that, in front of *our friends,* I'm going to have to put you in time out," she said with a light laugh.

Immediately Dallas's entire being flushed with relief.

"Yes, ma'm. Won't happen again," he said with a smirk as he settled his hand on her towel-clad hip.

"We meet with Amora in an hour. Badlands," he said as he inhaled her sweet woods and citrus meets vanilla cake scent mixed with motel shampoo.

"Right, the carnival," she said, making no move away from him. She only leaned in closer.

"I think you need to get dressed..." he commanded.

"I think you need to get on your

knees and do a little more groveling, first," she purred.

Dallas shook his head.

"Relentless," he said as he tugged at her towel with practiced force, before sliding to his knees just as she asked, just to show her how sorry he truly was.

And when Midnight threaded her fingers through his hair, when her energy *fed* him like a breakfast buffet as she came against his apologetic tongue, Dallas knew there was no place he'd rather be.

***

"What's this?" Dallas said as Amora slid him an ID.

He picked up the plastic card, glaring at the photograph of himself he wondered how she'd managed to get.

Though it read *Dallas Rainier*, and he wasn't sure what had possessed vampire Barbie to get him a fake ID, let alone one with two last names.

And so quickly...

Including a last name that belonged to his *mate.*

The word, *mate* had popped up in his psyche the prior night, when he'd been in the throes of passion with Midnight, driven by some otherworldly desire and need to possess this creature, this *woman* who called to his monstrous soul in a way he'd never felt before... and again that afternoon when he'd done his share of groveling, pleased as punch when his *mate* granted him the sweetest taste of forgiveness, and the word had been playing ping-pong in his brain ever since.

He understood what it meant, the levity of it, though he didn't know much more about bonded Djinn pairs except from the lore Hunter had brought them up to speed on several years ago, when they'd hunted their first Djinn.

His friend's words echoed in his brain as he remembered him telling how it was rare to find bonded Djinn. The nature of the creatures was to grant mortals deathwish, for it was the very thing they lived for, but they were mostly solitary creatures, unlike vampires. But even now, the ache Dallas once had for wishful thinking was vacant. He hungered instead for something else other than wishful thinking, other than blood.

"It was brought to my attention during my... discussion with Thomas

Mayfield and his allies, that you saved his friend's hide. A serendipitous accident, no doubt, but one that worked in our favor nonetheless," Amora said smoothly.

Dallas turned the plastic ID over, inspecting it with precision. In addition to being the most well learned man in the group of hunters, Hunter had more experience with false documents and IDs than a twenty-eight year old should have had. His skill and attention to detail had crafted many aliases for all of them over the years, thus Dallas knew the tells of poor identity falsifications.

He could not find a single stitch or marking that would have tipped anyone off. The ID was sound, and a damn good forgery.

"Why?" he asked, twirling the card in

between his large fingers. The Badlands was full of ghouls and Djinn, drinking, eating and chatting amongst themselves; the air in the place so different than it had been the night before, Dallas was convinced it was somewhere else altogether.

Amora cocked her head to the side, long, luscious blonde curls falling over her shoulder. She raised an eyebrow at him, her expression confused.

"Though it pains me to admit it, you have provided yourself useful, *Dallas*."

Her use of his name made his skin crawl, despite the fact her voice had darkened, and an air of seduction surrounded her like a fog.

As a mortal, he was more than capable of detecting and combating a vampire's thrall, but as a Djinn, the experience was far less threatening. The scent of lavender and lemons that filled the air between them reminded him of his grandmother's home in the summer, when he'd had nothing else to do except watch television and shoot Coke cans in the forest for fun.

"I didn't do it for you," he grunted.

Amora smiled, the sight somehow both beautiful and unsettling.

"I think you will find, Dallas, that I can be quite... giving to those I find valuable," she said as she took a step closer, her old lady scent making him feel rather nauseous.

"I'm not interested in what you have to give, *Amora*."

Amora traced her long, pink fingernail along his bicep, applying just a hair of pressure.

"I wouldn't discount my favor yet, my vicious little Viper. It is better to be my friend than my enemy. Just remember that," she said as she turned away, heading toward the group of Djinn and ghouls.

Dallas looked at the ID once more, running his finger over his newly assigned name, his stomach twisting with turmoil. He barely noticed as Boo came up beside him as Amora started her spiel about the carnival. But Dallas could barely focus.

"So you's official now, huh?" Boo said as he nudged Dallas's arm.

Dallas slid the ID in his pocket, pursing his lips.

"I'm not officially anything," he grumbled.

"Too bad, because I painted your

name on your bike while you was 'sposed to be *watching* Midnight on account of tha' venom an' all."

Dallas stood up straighter. "You what?"

Boo shrugged.

"Boy, if you was gonna run, you'd ran already." Boo turned to raise an eyebrow.

"And I certainly don't see you runnin' now that you've laid roots."

"I haven't laid anything," Dallas bit as he moved away from the lumbering Djinn who only snickered in his absence. Dallas's gaze fell to Midnight and Rebel, who sat at a table directly in front of Amora. Rebel picked at a plate of fries, but he'd noticed Midnight hadn't touched a single one.

In fact, he hadn't seen her eat

anything since they'd arrived in Kentucky.

Not to mention, he hadn't felt hungry for food himself, since they'd arrived either.

"And the carnival will commence in three days. That should give us enough time to build, spread the word. Our forces combined together outnumber the Boracellis. If we play our cards right, if you *listen to me,*" Amora said as she flashed her bright green eyes at Dallas, causing his skin to crawl once more.

"We will overthrow those blood-thirsty hounds and take their territory."

"What do the wolves have to say about that? Isn't this place *their* territory?*" A ghoul whose name Dallas hadn't bothered to learn, asked.

Amora smiled sweetly.

"If we take care of the Mayfield's *problem,* we will be rewarded handsomely."

Dallas stood up straighter.

"You mean if we kill the fucking *ticks,*" he said, enunciating the latter of his words, "for them, we get the territory."

"I'm glad to see you've been paying attention, Viper. Yes. Thomas Mayfield and I have come to an agreement on this. The goal was to always give my Heartsgrave a place to belong, a place where you can feast until your hearts content, where you can start anew."

Her words were saccharine, and the energy in the room shifted. Dallas could soon see faint aura lights emanating from every Djinn and ghoul in the room.

"You will finally be able to stop

running," she said with finality, her gaze holding his.

"Kill the Boracellis, and you can finally be free."

18

DALLAS TRAILED HIS lips over Midnight's collarbone, his fangs aching to bite, to taste her blood. He wondered momentarily if it would taste as sweet the rest of her. The overwhelming need to *possess* her, to bury himself inside of her until he ceased to exist was becoming much more pertinent every second he was away from her.

And after nearly twenty-four hours,

void of his scratch fever, he knew he no longer had an excuse.

The truth was evident as he shoved her black jeans to the ground around her ankles, the setting sun lighting up her bare ass as he wasted no time finding his entrance.

Midnight's head rolled forward against the neon-painted wall.

"Fuck," he groaned as he bottomed out, his right hand gripping her hips with more strength than he felt at the moment.

His left hand circled around to her front, finding her clit, tugging and pulling at the sensitive bead until Midnight's breath caught in her throat.

"Fuck... Faith... you feel so fucking good," he breathed, already feeling his release building at the base of his spine.

He hadn't even begun to move yet.

"Jake," she groaned as she arched her back, pushing against him as heat started to pool between them once more. The sound was music to his ears.

It had barely been twenty-four hours since they'd been bitten, since they'd crossed the line.

Since they *bonded.*

While he'd spent the last several hours assisting Boo and some of the other wolves—including Alaric—building and setting up the carnival rides and equipment, he'd felt a stark emptiness in the pit of his stomach. Midnight and Rebel had been tasked with look out duty on the other side of the fairgrounds, something that should have been absolutely fine, and not caused the vicious ache that it did to blossom within him.

He hated that his thoughts looped like a Ferris wheel, that even in her absence, all he could think about was her.

Her soft touch, her soothing voice, how perfect they fit together, and how complete and energized he felt after they toppled over the edge of ecstasy together as she held onto him, as her eyes closed and her mouth formed that perfect little 'o' in which she sung her praises.

As he walked across the grounds, the speakers blasted, filling the air with the sounds of Whitesnake's *Is This Love*, and the moment she'd entered his proximity, her thoughts filled his brain, his entire body awakening like a live wire, that magnetic pull too difficult to ignore. He'd followed it like a moth to a flame, if only to see her, kiss her, tell her despite all his better judgment that he... missed her. Even in his own brain, he knew it was insane to feel such a way in such a short span of time, but Dallas did not care about time.

And upon seeing her, behind the storage shed, his insides flared, the voice in his head echoing with truth.

Mine.

It was all a bit of a blur after that, as Midnight's eyes lit up upon seeing him, as she ran into his arms, her lips finding his in a flash of heat and fury as she pulled him behind the shed, her hands making deft work of finding his jeans and unbuckling his belt, as he responded to her need through their bond, through his hurried touch. The singer droned on and on about finding what he was searching for, but the sound was practically white noise to Dallas.

He teased her wet folds as he snapped his hips into her with a force that caused the wood of the shed to creak as he slammed her body against it. The sound only fed his energy, his desire as her energy mingled together with his.

The tiredness, the exhaustion he'd felt after lifting, screwing, and hoisting equipment all day in the hot sun fell away, replaced by an energy that left him feeling full in more ways than one.

"I'm so..."

His lips muffled midnight's words as he moved his hand up to her neck, grabbing it with enough force to turn her toward him to claim her words into his mouth.

I know. Me, too... His voice echoed in their shared consciousness, as intense waves of energy filled them both.

Midnight's insides pulsed around him as she moaned into his mouth without care, causing the chain reaction that he wanted to feel over and over again.

His vision went black as he stilled, dragging his hand from her sensitive clit back over her hip as he gently pulled her closer, filling her with his hot release, with wishful thoughts, promises, and... love?

"I love you," she whispered in his mouth.

The sound caused his entire body to stiffen, save for his throbbing, pulsing cock.

She broke away, looking up at him with eyes that were as vast as any ocean, the weight of those three little words immense in her gaze.

The fact he *wanted* to say it back was frightening, disorienting as he softened inside her.

"I—"

A sound beyond the shed startled them both, interrupting Dallas's fear, engaging his protective nature like a dormant spy.

He slid himself out of her warmth, hating the feel of the cool air against his wet cock, but the instinct of a threat nearby overrode everything else as he pulled his jeans up, before placing a hand at the small of her back.

"Stay here, Midnight," he said firmly.

She moved away from his touch only marginally, picking up her own crumpled clothing around her ankles, the air of heat between them still hanging in the air.

"Jake..." she said his name with worry as he turned to her, imploring her gaze.

"Stay here," he said, his tone darker.

"Don't argue with me."

The imperativeness of his tone must have been harsher than he intended, for Midnight pursed her lips, looking as if she was contemplating doing exactly the opposite. But she didn't.

"I'll be back, just... don't go anywhere, okay?" he asked, hating the vulnerability in his voice as it shook.

When had he become so... soft?

So pliable?

So easily swayed by pussy?

When you bonded yourself to another broken heart, that's when.

The reality of his internal realization both caused him to shiver and to feel much more bold as he slowly crossed the threshold of the fairground in the direction of the sound. It seemed to be coming from the fun house, which according Alaric, was one of the only pre-existing buildings that was left up all year round.

The sound of footsteps echoed in Dallas's ears, louder than it should have. But then again, he was no longer working with human hearing, and thus he could pinpoint the exact direction of the sound with precision.

Despite his monstrously new senses, the instinct, the natural inclination to hunt was just as it always was.

The scent of tobacco was prevalent in the air, mixed with leather and whiskey like a pungent cologne and Dallas stalked it across the edge of the fairgrounds just behind the back of the funhouse, where it stopped.

The sound of a blade being drawn alerted him, causing his blood to run cold as a familiar voice froze him.

"Give me one good fucking reason not to put this blade in your heart."

Dallas turned his head, his heart skipping an angered, frustrated beat of relief as his eyes settled on a leather-clad entity who held *his* blessed blade. The one he always left in the Chevelle in case of emergencies.

"Because if you wanted me fucking dead, Mal, you would've stabbed me already."

"Fuck you," Mal said, but he did not move an inch, and neither did Dallas.

Dallas smirked, sliding his hands in his pockets.

Mal let out a deep breath.

"Hands where I can fucking see them!" he said, his eyebrows furrowing.

It was then that Dallas noticed he was shaking.

He was afraid.

And something about that triggered the demons buried inside of Dallas, causing a tectonic shift in his own memories, his own emotion.

"Take it easy, Mal..."

"You're a fucking monster, Jake. Give me a reason not to fucking kill you."

The tears that begged to fall from his partner's face were the nail in his own proverbial coffin.

"Because I'm still me," he said softly.

"Give me a reason not to kill you

where you stand."

Malcolm ground his teeth together.

"You know if I wanted to hurt you I could. You wouldn't be standing if I wanted to kill you. I'm stronger now, better."

"You are not fucking better. You're a—"

"Monster? Yeah, we've established that. Now put the fucking knife down and maybe we can talk this out..."

"Since when do you want to talk about your fucking feelings?" Mal said, lowering his knife slowly.

Dallas breathed a sigh of relief.

For now.

"Because we have bigger problems than me being a fucking monster. A vamp problem. A hostage problem."

"I'm aware," Mal said as he crossed

his arms.

Dallas noted a flash of something in his eyes, something he'd never seen before and couldn't quite place. It looked a hell of a lot like the sparkle Midnight got in her eyes when she talked about her daughter, Emma.

"You on a hunt?" Dallas said as he slowly walked around the perimeter, keeping his distance, still unsure whether or not Mal was trying to trick him. The man was quite skilled and fast with a knife...

"Something like that," Mal responded, his gaze still wary.

"Then maybe we could work together. Like old times." Dallas decided to try a practical approach.

Malcolm seemed to consider his words.

"Aren't you already working with wolves? What do you need me for?" he said bitterly.

"How do you know about the wolves..." Dallas said, surprised.

"Like I said. You aren't the only one on a hunt, D."

"Maybe I don't trust the wolves, the way I trust you."

Mal shook his head, running his hand over his face.

"You shouldn't fucking trust me, not for a second." Mal sighed, turning around.

"You're right, I shouldn't. Given you lured me here to fucking stab me," Dallas grunted, crossing his arms. They'd come closer together, despite trying to stay away.

Mal's shoulders fell as Dallas spoke.

"You've always had my back, Mal, and I've always had yours. Rule number one."

Mal turned around.

"What about your new band of brothers, huh? You got their backs too, now? They your new family?"

Malcolm's words cut Dallas to the core.

"No. Some bonds are stronger than blood, Mal," he said, the truth heavy in the air between them.

"Meet me back here at midnight. If you're really serious, come alone."

Mal turned around, heading for the forest.

"Midnight it is," Dallas said as he walked away, a sense of fear overtaking him.

Because for the first time, he wasn't

sure where Malcolm's loyalties lay.

19

MIDNIGHT FELT ON edge. While their tryst against the storage shed had left her feeling sated and full in many ways, it had also left her feeling rather vulnerable and exposed.

She'd told Jake Dallas that she *loved* him. She knew in her being it was true, the words themselves felt right, like an entity of its own once breathed into existence.

They'd bonded as Djinn on a mate level, but also on a *human* level.

She'd felt his trauma, his pain and heartache, as it echoed her own. In the shared space between such awful, dire things, they found love in a hopeless place. A dark place, and together they formed a ray of light. He'd promised her a *heartswish* for goodness sakes, a promise that was beyond powerful and only contrastable to a deathwish.

But he hadn't said it back, and Midnight knew it wasn't because they had been interrupted.

A part of her understood he hadn't said the words likely since... since he'd lost *her.* His wife. He didn't seem the type to throw romantic words around meaninglessly. But it didn't dilute the desire within her that she wanted to hear them. *Needed* to hear them because no one had said them to her in honesty.

When he returned, he seemed different. Standoffish, even.

"I'll see you later tonight? At the Badlands?" she asked as they came to the edge of the concessions, where Boo and some wolves were working on assembling a ride of parachutes.

Thomas Mayfield had extended his hospitality to the wolves 'new allies', and Midnight and the others were not going to refuse such hospitality. Especially when it came to alcohol and food.

Not that she'd been hungry as of late.

"What the hell crawled up your ass and died?" Rebel said between bites of cheeseburger.

Midnight picked at the side portion of

fries in front of her. The sight and smell disgusted her, despite the fact she used to love them.

"I fucked up, Reby." She sighed, pushing the plate away.

"Are we talking about your appetite or..."

"You know what I mean," she said.

Or rather, who.

Rebel set her cheeseburger down, a stoic look on her face.

"You're going to tell me regardless if I want to hear it or not, so just get on with it, Midnight," she said as she sat back with a raised eyebrow.

Midnight groaned, chewing on her fingernail.

"I may have said something... preemptively."

"Let me guess, you professed your

undying love to Tall, Dark, and Stupid, and suddenly he's an icebox."

Midnight groaned, realizing at her friend's words it sounded worse out loud.

Fuck, how could I have been so stupid!

Rebel's expression softened, as if she, too, could read her mind.

"Hey. We've all been there, sweetheart. It's like asshole 101," she said with a smirk.

"I mean, who hasn't been railed to the point of spouting Shakespeare because the dick was *that* good." Rebel laughed.

Midnight groaned, settling her head in her hands.

This was a bad idea. I need to stay focused on more important things. Like finding Emma.

"I mean, it's not like you *actually* love him or anything," Rebel said as she pulled a fry from Midnight's plate.

"I know it's crazy, Reby but—"

"Aw shit, Midnight, don't tell me you're falling for this asshole," Rebel scoffed.

Midnight dropped her hands, looking her friend in the eye.

"I wish I could say no, but... it just... it all kinda happened so fast, and then we bonded, and then—"

"You what?" Rebel hollered, drawing the attention of a group of ghouls from nearby.

"We... bonded."

"How? You're both unbound, you're... He didn't bite you, did he? Did you bite him? Fuck, Midnight..."

She hadn't remembered shedding any

blood, but the reality of Rebel's words echoed as the memory of his teeth in the flesh of her lip broke forth.

The tiniest taste of blood in her mouth was like a cold splash of water.

Could it have been enough to cement a bond?

She hadn't tasted his blood...

"I mean, I knew something was different because I could hear him, and his wishful thinking since that night we found him at the Marquis, and then when he sang, his energy fed me, and when we... it wasn't like a bite, bite. Just a nip, and I didn't bite him..."

"Oh fuck, Midnight." Rebel sighed in defeat.

"You're absolutely sure, you didn't have any of his blood?"

"No," she said, the answer leaving her

feeling even emptier. The word *blood* caused her mouth to water, her insides to tighten as the thought of sinking her fangs into Dallas's skin as he drove her over the edge into oblivion filled her psyche.

But it was only wishful thinking... since he hadn't said a word since he'd left her to help Boo and the wolves. Her gaze traveled across the Badlands, falling on the clock that read eleven fifty pm.

He said he would be here...

"Then it's not complete. You still have time to reverse it."

The words stopped her heart.

"I don't want to reverse it, Rebel. I want..."

"What about him, Midnight? Does he know what a bond entails? Did you tell him? Or did you just forget, because you were too focused on getting yourself off?"

Midnight growled, turning away from her friend.

"It's not like that. Our bond is different, it's not just sex."

"Sure it's not, honey." Rebel shrugged, pulling Midnight's fries to her side of the table.

"Love can't be forced, Midnight. No matter what species we are." Rebel sighed.

"That's why I avoid getting attached. It just makes things messy."

Midnight stood from her table.

"I think I've lost my appetite altogether," she said as she walked away.

"Midnight, come on..." Rebel called out, but Midnight did not answer.

Instead, she walked through the cold air across the lot toward the hotel, giving up on the conversation, on Jake Dallas's disappearance, all of it.

She had bigger things to worry about, and she needed to focus and keep her eye on the prize.

***

It was nearly two-thirty when the door to the motel opened. Midnight did not turn around, did not open her eyes. She just continued to lay motionless on the bed, wrapped up in the sheets like a black and pink bunny clad burrito.

The sounds of Foreigner from her phone droning about wanting to know love filled the otherwise quiet space. The song always soothed her, the same way it had soothed Emma when she'd sing it to her when she was restless.

The bed creaked from the weight of Dallas as he sat down. It seemed an eternity until he pulled his legs up on the bed, turning beside her. Yet he did not touch her, and she hated that her body *yearned* for his touch. He was so close, yet so far away.

She kept her eyes closed, trying to hold back the tears that threatened to fall. Memories of Emma's tiny fist clutching her shoulder, of her soft yawns as she paraded her around the dark cabin amidst rainy days filled her with longing.

Memories of Emma's cute voice as she tried to pronounce band names like Whitesnake or her favorite, Bananarama, in which Emma just called Bannanana endlessly.

The mate bond between them flared with intensity, the sliver of space somehow cavernous even though it was anything but.

Dallas handed her a small piece of paper. It took her a moment to realize what it was, her heart stopping at the sight.

"Where did you get this?" she asked with panic, her fingers straightening the edges of her photograph. The one she kept tucked into her wallet.

"Found it on the floor by the door. Thought you might want to put it somewhere safe." His voice was soft, even.

She ran her fingertips over the faded, crinkled spots in the same way she always did, hoping, wishing with each stroke that somehow Emma could feel her love.

That she knew she'd come for her.

"She's a beauty, just like her mom," Dallas said with a soft smile.

Midnight's heart felt as if it would explode out her chest altogether.

"Thank you," she said with awe.

Despite being the father of her child, Trevor had never once called her or Emma beautiful, and the levity of that was not lost on her.

She'd been desperate for Trevor Boracelli and his elusive love, his attention, to make something out of nothing.

"What was it like?" Dallas asked, his voice full of sadness.

"What was what like?" she whispered as she set the photograph down on her nightstand, beneath the clock radio.

Dallas breathed a heavy sigh beside her.

"What did it feel like to... hold her?" he asked shakily.

Midnight turned to look at Dallas with his arms around his knees, wearing only his boxers, his golden skin almost amber in the low light of the motel room. His naturally bright eyes were full of sadness, and his pain echoed inside of her.

She debated answering him, but resistance was futile. She only longed to soothe his soul, to give him the closure, the space he needed to breathe. To grieve all that he had lost and move forward.

And perhaps, she needed to do the same, to put Trevor and his ugly love behind her, once and for all.

"Perfect. Like despite all the mistakes I made, somehow I managed to get something right."

"How old is she?" he asked.

"Well, this was taken when she was four, right before she was taken, so she'd be eight, going on nine next week."

Dallas only nodded.

"Kelly would have been turning sixteen this winter," he said as he let his legs out.

"If Laura would have made it to her assigned due date. December fifth."

His words didn't waver, but his energy reached out for her. It called to her, begging to be touched, to be held.

To be *loved*.

Midnight looked up at him from where she lay. There were a hundred things she wanted to say, questions she wanted to ask. But all she could settle on was, "Hell, can you imagine? You? With a teenager? You'd have your hands full."

Dallas shot her a smirk that warmed her to her core.

"I was really looking forward to chasing some idiot up the hill, like Laura's dad chased my ass."

Midnight let out a chuckle.

"I would have loved to have seen that."

"Not a day goes by I don't wonder what my life would have been like if..." He turned away, his shoulders falling with his deep sigh.

Midnight scooted closer, setting her hand on his, where it rested above his knee.

"If things had been different," he said

quietly.

"I know the feeling," she said as he set his hand over top of hers.

"I made you a promise, Faith. We'll get her back."

Midnight sat up, her black shirt falling off her shoulder from the motion. The seriousness in his voice and in his gaze was full of unspoken words.

"You said *we.*" Her voice was small, full of hope.

Dallas slid his hand across her cheek, his fingers sliding into her tangled, messy bun. He shook his head absentmindedly.

"I did, didn't I?" he breathed, his breath warm against her skin.

Mate.

The word echoed in their shared consciousness, in the synchronized beat of their hearts.

She nodded softly as he pulled her closer into the space between his legs, his lips brushing against hers with a softness, a tenderness that spoke volumes beyond tangible words.

Yes, their bond was more than something physical.

It was spiritual, it was magical, and it was *theirs*.

In the wreckage of their lives, they'd found something to live for.

Something neither of them thought they'd ever have again.

Midnight kissed him slowly, savoring the taste of him, his intoxicating scent, his warm touch.

And when he broke away, he held her closer, and he whispered, "I'm sorry."

"There's nothing to be sorry for,

Jake," she assured him, and perhaps she was also assuring herself.

"I hope you're right, Faith. I fucking hope you are right."

****

Dallas's hands trailed over Midnight's abdomen as he placed a kiss on her neck, his fangs brushing her skin. The sting of his bite filled her with so much relief, so much fulfillment, Midnight thought she may explode into a thousand pieces.

He rocked his hips, thrusting deeper as she met his rhythm, his blood in her mouth sweet and full of heartswish, of wishful thinking, and of hopes and dreams.

"Mine," she purred as she raked her nails down his chest, blood trailing

behind her fingertips.

"You belong to me now..." she said as she licked his blood from her lips.

Dallas looked up at her with stars in his eyes, and the world fell away...

A warm, tight embrace, and a solid, rigid cock poking at her behind roused Midnight awake.

Her panties were soaked, her body warm with sweat, and her insides *throbbing* with the need to be filled, to be bound.

She looked at the clock on the nightstand, which read nearly two o clock in the afternoon.

I've been asleep for twelve hours... I can't remember the last time I slept like this...

Dallas grumbled as his hand slid over her hip, across her stomach, his fingers teasing the hem of her pajama pants.

Her insides fluttered from the touch, and she sighed contentedly.

She rather liked how they fit together, her small frame nuzzled in his much larger one like a safe cocoon.

She burrowed into his hold a little more, not wanting to get up. Her body was just as exhausted as her mind, and she was *starving*.

"Good morning," she whispered as she turned in his grasp to see his bright eyes staring back at her.

He leaned in to kiss her, pulling her closer as he ground his cock into her from the motion itself.

"Good morning, Cinderella," he purred groggily, the sarcasm in his tired voice somehow endearing.

"Today's a big day," she said as she

traced his jaw with her fingertips.

He is body tensed for a moment.

"What?" he said, much more alert.

"The run through for the plans for tomorrow? The carnival?" she said, reminding him.

His shoulders eased.

"Yeah, of course. I knew that. Just tired... is all."

"Me, too. Tired and hungry," she said with a smirk as she slid her hand down between them, wrapping her hand around his clothed erection.

"Fucking relentless," he said as he shook his head, his lips finding hers once more.

"You sure you're a Djinn and not some long lost breed of nymph?" he teased.

Midnight giggled, shaking her head as

Dallas kissed her with a mouthful of laughter, using his form to roll her over so that he was on top of her, looking down at her with sparkling ocean eyes full of light and happiness. It was a most beautiful sight to behold and she wanted to see more happiness on his face.

"Don't act like you don't love it," she teased. Dallas leaned over her, running his fingers through her hair.

"Shit, am I that easy?" he purred, his voice some mixture of cockiness and playfulness that caused her own energy to ebb. His happiness and love radiated out of him like the sun as he slid her pajamas off slowly, his gaze never leaving hers.

Midnight smiled brightly.

"Naw, I'm just that good," she said with a smirk as she watched Dallas free his cock above her.

The sunlight shone on him like an angel, lighting him up in shades of gold and ochre like he was Apollo himself.

Like he was everything she'd wished for.

Dallas single-handedly her panties.

"You didn't say please," he purred against her neck.

"Please," she moaned as her lips found his.

Dallas's lips curled up into a smile as he sucked at her bottom lip, his tongue grazing hers softly.

"Your wish is my command," he teased, as he slid into her wetness with ease, his warmth and energy taking over her body, her mind, and her heart.

Midnight held on for dear life. Her body welcomed him and his warmth. For

Dallas moved his hips so slowly, the drag of his hardness and smooth rhythm so torturous; she could have sworn it was a form of punishment.

She wanted more.

She wanted every bit of this man, her mate, that he was willing to give her.

"Faster," she purred, her voice edged with deep longing.

"Please," she begged, egging him on as she tilted her hips to meet his.

Dallas ran his fingers through her hair softly, staring down at her with a glaze in his eyes that looked almost like tears. But surely that wasn't the case.

Men didn't cry during sex.

Her insides clutched his thickness like a vice as he slid out of her almost to the point of a full exit before slowly thrusting into her once more, a fraction deeper, driving her innate desire wild. He let out a deep, shaky breath as he repeated the motion swiftly, rocking her into the soft, crumpled sheets and pillows. Her orgasm swelled within her.

"I want to take my time," he said as his lips claimed hers in a gentle, sweet kiss.

"I don't want to rush," he whispered softly in her mouth. His hands slid down her thighs as he brought her leg up, wrapping it around his hip, the angle only forging him deeper into her, into the bond they shared until she could see the stars in his eyes.

"Faith, look at me," he whispered, his forehead settled against hers.

Like an obedient child, she met his command without a second thought.

His words shattered Midnight as he

spoke them.

"I need you to feel this," he said shakily as he took her hand, sliding it over his heart.

The steady, slow beat echoed her own and she felt moisture prickling the edges of her eyes as well.

"Tell me," he whispered, his eyes shimmering like sapphires, like starry nights.

"Tell me you can feel this," he said, his voice screwed up, caught in his throat. The intensity of his words washed over her like a balm, soothing her soul.

And at that moment, Midnight knew it didn't matter if she bit him, if he bit her, if he showed up or didn't show up when he said he would, his past, his future, none of it mattered, because despite all of it, she could feel the words he longed to say, but was afraid to in the present as his heart beat beneath her palm.

She could feel his love.

She could see it hiding in the edges of his bright eyes.

She could feel it in his kiss, his touch, hear it in their shared space.

She nodded as he settled his elbows beside her, his right hand stroking her hair with a gentleness a man like him should not have been capable of. He kept his pace, slow and steady, his thrusts in tandem with her racing heartbeat until Midnight was nothing but sensation, her release so close, but yet so far on the horizon.

His left hand gripped her thigh as he stared down at her. The angle as he clutched her, drove him deeper, and she wrapped both her legs around him, her arms reaching up around his neck, pulling him closer, their lips brushing for a moment as she whispered honestly, "I feel *you*, Jake, in every part of me."

The moment they collided, all heated kisses and tangled limbs and synchronized heartbeats, all love and hope, the world became brighter.

And when Dallas finally left her body, heading for the shower, only then did Midnight realize she was no longer starving.

20

"FOR A MINUTE there, I thought maybe you'd changed your mind," Malcolm said as he emerged from the shadows.

Dallas wrinkled his nose.

"You smell like wet dogs."

Malcolm flipped him off.

"And you smell like the clearance aisle of Bath and Body Works, but you don't see me complaining."

Dallas grumbled.

"I can't help that, it's just part of the fucking DNA."

Mal shrugged.

"Yeah, well neither can I. It's part of..."

Dallas didn't miss the way Malcolm's eyes widened and he abruptly coughed, as if he was avoiding being truthful.

"Part of what? Your nightly werewolf orgy?" Dallas bit as they reached the edge of the perimeter.

"No!" Mal answered, a bit too defensively.

Guess I'm not the only one who likes supernatural pussy.

Dallas shook his head as Mal handed him a phone.

"What's this?"

"I mean, I haven't gotten a hit off your phone in a week, so I assumed it's deader than you should probably be."

Mal held the phone out like some sort of olive branch, but Dallas couldn't be certain it was such.

He knew Malcolm Crowley was smart. He tracked everything.

Could he trust that this wasn't some form of deception?

"It's not bugged," he said as if he was capable of reading Dallas's thoughts.

"But we're going to have to have some form of communication. I'm not well versed in smoke signals."

Dallas grabbed the phone, turning it over in his hand.

"Phone's smashed to pieces. Never got it fixed," he said, sliding it in his back pocket. The sun filtered through the trees, the heat of midday in Kentucky already hitting a fever pitch.

"Didn't have time with everything else going on..."

Malcolm gave a slight nod.

"Right," he said as he shut the trunk of the Chevelle and they both headed into the woods.

The silence between them was thick and full of tension.

His entire body felt the distance between him and his mate.

Faith.

Though Dallas understood that to the rest of The Heartsgrave she was purely Midnight, as he was *Viper*—a name he was starting to grow to like for the ferocity of its sound—he found himself wanting to say *her* name over and over again.

It tumbled off his tongue so easily, the sound warm and soft, like velvet.

Even now, miles away, his energy called for her, his wishful thoughts straying to her bright eyes and the sound of her laugh. Faith had a *beautiful* laugh, and he wanted to hear more of it.

His muscles were tight, his insides twisting, cold and in need of the warmth that only seemed to come from the closeness he felt when he was wrapped around her body, when he filled her.

In all his years, he'd never felt so deeply connected to anyone. Not his wife, not Ava...

Ava.

The realization he hadn't thought about her, that he'd almost *forgotten* her completely left him feeling conflicted. His words betrayed him.

"How are the others?" His voice was solid and did not waver, but his entire body tensed when he felt the desire to say her name.

Ava...

Malcolm side-eyed him as they picked up the pace, traipsing through the shadowed wood where only days ago he'd been bitten by a werewolf, where he'd discovered so much more than what he was made of...

"I didn't tell them the truth if that's what you're asking. As far as they know you're dead. Like you are supposed to be," Mal said, his voice etched in pain and anger.

"And Ava?" he asked as they came to a stop.

Mal looked at him, letting out a deep, frustrated breath.

"Well, she's not drunk anymore, so that's a plus."

Dallas winced at his former partner's words.

"Fuck, Mal—"

"She's taken up stabbing anything that moves, which is a far better approach than bawling her eyes out."

"And you're chasing monsters instead of taking care of her."

Mal leaned in close, his eyes full of fury.

"Don't fucking do that. Don't act like for one fucking second you give a shit about what happens to my *sister*. I should kill you right now where you fucking stand."

"Then why don't you?" Dallas said as he challenged Mal's space.

"Huh? You want to put that blade in my chest to make yourself feel better? So you don't have to fucking lie to her?

You'll find something else, Mal. Something else to keep from her, you always do."

Mal held his blade to Dallas's throat.

"I guess you know a thing or two about secrets considering you were fucking my sister behind my damn back.'

Dallas gripped the blade, pushing back against it.

"It wasn't anyone's business but ours," he said.

"Stay the fuck away from her," Mal said, his eyes glassy.

"I have no intention of hurting Ava, Mal. Just like I don't want to hurt you." He pushed the blade down, staring back at the man he'd called his brother for over a decade.

"I just want to do something good for

a change," Dallas said honestly.

Mal dropped his hand and blade to his side.

"We always did good, D."

"Did we though? What did it get us? Fuck, Mal, what did it get you?" Dallas asked as he continued to walk.

"Fucking Djinn DNA is messing with your damn head, Dallas."

"No, Mal. I'm seeing shit clearly for the first time, and not everything is as black and white as you think it is."

"I'll take the left. You take the right," Mal said as they came to the edge of the vampire's estate.

In the sunlight it didn't look quite as menacing.

It almost looked like the perfect place to raise a family. A place where the pitter patter of bare feet ran rampant up and down wooden steps, where rain storms would echo in the hallways from their cascade on the roof, where the scent of fresh brewed sweet tea clung to everything including the linens.

It looked like the kind of place Dallas had always dreamed about when he was a young wide receiver, that he hoped he'd have one day to share with his wife and kids.

But the vampires weren't holding their prisoners here out of love and appreciation, and Dallas pushed all thoughts of such things out of his mind as he pulled out the tiny photograph he'd swiped from Midnight's nightstand.

He'd hunted many things in his time as a human, content with the life of living out of motels and cars, singing metal covers, and enjoying the slivers of attachment in between it all. The moments where Ava forgot she was supposed to keep him out, instead of let him in.

But none of those things mattered anymore.

In just the span of eight or nine days, Jake Dallas had become someone else. A moth emerged from the cocoon of his former self, and as he ran his thumb over the torn edge of Emma's picture, he had to admit he no longer wanted to live a life of blood and death.

This is the last hunt.

He promised himself as he shoved the photograph back in his pocket, as he walked into the sun, that come hell or high water, he would find a way to make his new existence something *good.*

He may have been a monster in

blood, but he didn't have to be one in practice. The choice was his own, and that day Dallas made his own heartswish.

He only hoped that he would live to see it granted.

***

Dallas looked around the fairgrounds, feeling quite like an imposter.

Though the carnival had attracted quite a large crowd as Thomas and Alaric claimed it would, it was the first time since he'd nearly drained his first victim that he'd been around humans.

It's only been a little over a week, how does it feel like months?

Like years?

The distinction that he was no longer one of them—human—caused his anxiety to swell. He was not one of them, but he was not quite the enemy, either. Not like the vamps that had decided to stick their flag in Mayfield, and refused to budge and make way for The Heartsgrave, who snatched up *children* for their nefarious bloodthirsty agenda.

Whatever that agenda was, didn't matter. All that mattered was getting into that estate and rescuing those kids.

Rescuing Emma.

He looked at the humans strolling through the grassy field eating their cotton candy and laughing, watching their kids run in line for rides that were one malfunction away from being a deathtrap, and felt a sense of protectiveness for them, the same sense he always had when he'd been on the other side of things. When he'd been a hunter, hunting monsters. Taking down the bad guys.

But as he walked with his hands in his pockets toward The Whip, his eyes peeled and senses heightened in expectation for the bloodsuckers, waiting for the right time to enact the plan he and Malcolm had hatched, Dallas knew he'd only have one shot.

With Djinn everywhere, they'd trap the vampires easily, and with Amora's no surprise attack rule, it would be easy to keep tails on them, especially if they were hungry.

All they needed was one vampire in the funhouse. One vampire who was hungry enough to sequester a poor, unfortunate human to the enticing fun house.

Boo would make sure the victim—or

rather the bait—got to safety, giving Dallas ample time to do what hey did best. And he would relish in tormenting the fucking tick until it sang like a bird and told him what the vamps wanted with the kids, and where to find them.

Then he'd text Malcolm, meet him at the estate, and do what they did best.

Save people from the monsters.

But he hated lying to Midnight.

I'm doing this for her.

He fought to keep the thoughts to himself, a notion that had become far too difficult in the past forty-eight hours.

Because you're bonded now. You've let her in.

Dallas stopped, leaning his hands over the railing as he watched The Whip snap around the corner, watched the kids in the cars smoosh one another as laughter erupted from their throats.

He hadn't given much thought to after, because in his line of work, it was best not to plan too far ahead. Plans went awry, obstacles came up. Dallas was used to only dealing with the problem, the case in front of him.

After they'd done what they came to do, his hunter friends and he would celebrate. Usually with drinks, music, pool, and pussy.

But none of that felt like who he was. It only felt like a memory, a ghost of a life he lived because he was lost, searching for the next best thing to take the pain away.

"One last hunt," he murmured aloud, hearing the finality of his words.

"Even if it kills me."

"If what kills you?" Midnight's voice

pulled him from his thoughts, and he immediately tensed.

The sight of her dressed in her usual black jeans and tank top, styled with an oversized leather jacket, reminded him of someone else. Her long, black hair flowed down her shoulders, crimson lips standing out against her pale flesh. She looked like a pretty, badass version of a leather-clad Snow White.

And Dallas knew with absolute certainly that she belonged to him, now, just as he belonged to her.

And for the moment, that was enough to soothe his internal storms and quiet the anxiety swelling within him.

"Nothing, just thinking about what I wouldn't give for a fucking corn dog right now," he lied easily.

Midnight raised an eyebrow.

"We've got an hour to kill until sundown. What's stopping you?" she asked as she joined him where he stood, leaning against the rail. Dallas's eyes roved over her.

"Nothing, I guess." He swallowed.

"Come on, let's feed your demon. You can grab me an ice cream while you're at it."

Dallas smirked.

"Let me guess, you're a chocolate lover."

Midnight wrinkled her nose.

"Actually no, I hate chocolate."

"You really are a fucking monster," he teased her as she playfully smacked his arm.

"Maybe I just have better taste than you," she said as he lunged for her. She jumped just out of his reach, dancing backward.

"Relentless," he said as he chased after her, through the crowds, feeling like he was some teenager, lost in the echo of a perfect summer night.

He finally caught her just on the edge of the patch of ground that had been turned into a make shift dance floor, the sound of Whitney Houston singing about dancing and heat filling the space as he pulled Midnight into his arms.

"Can't outrun a hunter, Bambi."

She eased into his hold, melting into his arms like butter.

"Maybe I want to be caught," she teased as she leaned up on her tiptoes. The height put her just a few inches below his lips.

"Maybe I just like it when you chase me," she said as she bit her lip.

"You just like to push my fucking buttons," he breathed, rocking her back and forth to the rhythm of the music. Amidst the standing purple and pink lights, she looked stunning.

He settled his right hand at the small of her back, his left pushing some soft hair behind her ear as the words threatened to erupt out of him like a volcano.

"Faith, I—" His words disappeared in the air as his gaze fell on the sight of a child behind her, across the way, in the crowd, surrounded by equally beautiful beings who carried themselves with a sophistication that was clearly embedded in them from another time.

A child whose brownish-blonde hair and almost crimson eyes stood out to him even at such a distance as they were. Her pale features were softer, but reminiscent of her mother in her bone structure and the shape of her eyes, and she looked almost angelic, despite her unnatural eyes.

Which were green in the photo.

His entire body went still as he focused on keeping up a wall between him and Midnight, if only not to alarm her, for Dallas knew Midnight would take off like a bat out of hell, and potentially put herself in danger, given the ring of vampires surrounding her daughter. And he just couldn't let that happen. He needed to protect her. After all, they had nearly killed her once already...

He understood at once that she was not entirely human as his eyes met Emma's. A part of him wanted to rage against the *lie* he'd been told, because that changed everything... didn't it?

Vampires aren't born anymore... not to mention, Faith was human when she had Emma... How could this happen?

Midnight's fingers played with the edges of his hair, her voice soft and understanding, oblivious to the fact her daughter was only ten feet away.

It took everything in Dallas to keep his face from baring the expression that would ruin both the woman he was falling in love with, and the chance to give her the heartswish he promised.

"It's okay, Jake. I know," she said, sliding her hand over his neck and collarbone, down to the spot over his right star tattoo.

Dallas regrettably tore his gaze from Emma to focus on Midnight. He wanted to be angry.

Maybe she didn't know...

But even as he thought the words, as he looked in her eyes, he knew that wasn't the case.

A mother always knows. Which meant she'd kept the truth from him.

What else had she lied about?

His heart beat slowly beneath her warm palm, her bright energy feeding his starved, worried soul.

She was protecting her. Because I hunt monsters, and her daughter is one of them.

There was a time Dallas would not have blinked at such revelations. Monsters were monsters, that was just the way it was. It was a distinction that was black and white. There was no grey area.

But monstrous children were something he'd never encountered in all his years on the road hunting things that went bump in the night.

His training told him that Emma was dangerous. The lore of bloodborn vampires stated that such abominations needed to transition to become the bloodsuckers that undoubtedly prayed on mortals and discarded them like utter trash.

Under the guise of vampires for four years... who was to say she wasn't brainwashed by the blood-thirsty bastards?

That she wouldn't try and hurt him or Midnight?

What if she didn't remember her mother?

For the first time in his life, he was

conflicted. The man he was would have called up Malcolm, told him the truth. They would have hatched a plan together. Probably burned up the building full of vamps to prevent anyone from murdering innocents in the future.

Emma smiled, and it was the same smile Midnight wore on her beautiful face, and Dallas knew he was no longer the man he used to be.

Because when he looked at Emma, he did not see a monster.

He only saw a child who needed to be saved.

Dallas let out a heavy breath as he looked in Midnight's eyes, the bright glow of aquamarine that distinguished her as a creature of wishes and blood, he knew there was only one thing to say, one thing to do.

So he focused on fixing his expression, on holding the wall in their consciousness, and he pretended he hadn't just seen the one thing he knew would shatter Midnight Rainier's world into pieces.

"You should head over to concessions," he said with a smile.

"I'll meet up with you in a few, I just need to hit a bathroom," he lied.

To his surprise, Midnight bought it, hook, line, and sinker.

"Okay," she said, with a sweet smile of her own as she pushed away from him, out of his arms.

He hated the emptiness that followed as he watched her walk off, and when she was out of sight altogether, only then did Dallas embark on his final hunt.

21

IT HAD BEEN more than twenty minutes, and Midnight was starting to worry. Something was wrong, she could feel it in her bones. The air thickened and she smelled blood.

Dallas had said he'd be right back, but she couldn't wait. The smell of blood and all it carried was sweet in the air, and it tempted her in a way it hadn't since... since she'd met the handsome hunter-turned Djinn. Before, she'd fed on her share of it, even though she didn't like how messy it was.

It smelled like *heaven.*

She preferred to soak up her meals through song, but doing so usually required a bit of planning ahead, and it wasn't always easy to find karaoke bars in the middle of nowhere, not to mention most mortals would look at a woman randomly belting out songs in public as a lunatic. She could charm one or two individuals, but a group or a room was beyond her capabilities.

No, she'd done as the rest of the women in The Heartsgrave had done. She lured men with her body, her beauty, with her promise to fulfill their lustful wishes until she'd cornered them like a spider and feasted on their wishful thinking, giving them just a taste of the addictive deathwish that would land them in Amora's deceptive web to be devoured.

But Dallas was not here, and she was caught between concern, and a strangely painful hunger pang.

And so Midnight gave into curiosity and abandoned her post, following the scent of blood like the scent of hot funnel cakes.

With icing.

That sounds really good about right now...

"Midnight, what are you doing over here? Aren't you supposed to be at the Cat Rack?" Boo's voice stopped her in her tracks.

She turned to face her friend, in the low light of oncoming dusk. Something seemed... off.

Maybe I'm the one who's off today...

"I just... I was hungry," she said, heat washing over all of a sudden, causing a sweat to form on her skin beneath her clothes. She took off her jacket, relishing in the cold air. The humid Kentucky heat was getting to her.

"That makes two of us, sweetheart. Come on, let's go get something to eat before all hell breaks loose," Boo said as he held his hand out.

Midnight looked at her friend, as the pain in her stomach radiated upward, spreading like a venom to her heart.

"Something's wrong, Boo," she said, feeling panic set in.

Flashes tore through her mind, darkness, shadows... blood.

So much blood.

The sight elicited a deep pain and she braced herself against the pillar by the edge of the ice cream concession.

"Come on, Midnight, let's go..."

"I can't, I—" Midnight's eyes closed as another pang of heat and pain pulsed through her, the smell of blood in the air and the sight of it over tan, thick muscles making her both hungry and nauseous all at once.

Find Malcolm Crowley.

Dallas's voice was strained in their shared consciousness and Midnight clutched her stomach as she tried to breathe through the pain.

I fucked up. I'm sorry... I...

Midnight's eyes widened as reality set in. Her throat radiated with pain as if she'd been bitten, and all at once she understood.

Dallas was in pain, therefore she was in pain.

Because they were bound.

"Boo, Dallas is hurt." Midnight forced the words through her teeth.

"I can feel it. I can feel him…"

"Come on Midnight. We needs ta get you somewhere safe, sweetheart." Boo pulled her close, hugging her tightly as he held her upright. Midnight felt a slight pinch at her neck, trying to process the echo of pain amidst what felt like her own.

Like she'd been bitten.

Rebel appeared just beyond the forest line, catching her gaze.

"There you are, Midnight, I've been looking everywhere for you!" Rebel said in exasperation.

It was only a moment until she was in

front of them.

"She's talking nonsense. I think she's—"

"I'll get her from here, Boo," Rebel said, her voice stern, commanding.

"I—"

Rebel's eyes glowed as she spoke slowly, hypnotically.

"I said, I got her from here, big guy. Go to your post." Rebel's voice was like silk.

"Of course," Boo said, nodding like he'd been possessed. Or charmed...

"Good boy," Rebel purred as Midnight watched Boo walk off, feeling a sense of panic lacing through her. Nothing made sense, and everything hurt.

Rebel looked down at Midnight with bright eyes, a wave of relaxation falling over Midnight like a hazy blanket.

"Looks like you're starting the party without me. Boo's right, though, we should get you somewhere safe. Somewhere that fucking asshole can't hurt you. I told you, you couldn't trust him," Rebel said as she wrapped her arms around her friend, holding her for support.

"Reby..."

Midnight's eyes felt heavy.

Midnight felt compelled to do as her friend asked. Like charmspeak...or thrall. Exhaustion befell her, and moving her legs was difficult. Her gaze fell on the tiny, almost indistinguishable drop of blood at the corner of Rebel's lips.

And that was the last thing Midnight saw before darkness pulled her under in the arms of woman she once called her friend.

22

DALLAS FOLLOWED EMMA and her captors through the crowd of unsuspecting, oblivious mortals until they'd disappeared into thin air. He cursed himself, looking every which way, expecting to find them, but it was no use. He cursed himself as he kicked a nearby trashcan, heat radiating through his body.

He'd been so close. So fucking close...

And he'd lost her.

Think, Dallas, think.

He waltzed back and forth, wracking his brain as to what to do. He contemplated finding Midnight, but could he look her in the eye knowing he'd failed to do what he promised?

Impulse gave way to reason. He'd hunted vamps before, this was no different.

But as he did so, he knew it was indeed different, and so he continued to walk, continued to channel his best Malcolm Crowley and think the situation through. His hand in his pocket fell over his burner phone and he pulled it out, looking at it with trepidation. There was *one* option.

I could call Mal... tell him the truth...

The thought permeated his brain,

causing his protective instincts to flare into overdrive.

But how can I trust he won't do what he's trained to do?

How can I trust that he won't hurt Emma because of what she is if once I was willing to do the same...

Dallas slid his phone back in his pocket as he kept walking in the woods, trying to think of something to say to Midnight, trying to think of a simple solution to a complicated matter.

He noticed the smell of blood before he heard the sound of the rustling bush.

Perhaps this will be easier than I thought...

He turned to see Rebel standing just several feet away.

"Fuck, Rebel... you nearly gave me a heart attack."

"Shouldn't you be at your post, *Viper?*" she asked coldly.

"It's not even dark yet. Vamps won't be out until it is."

"You know, I expected that a hunter would know *some* vampires do have the ability to exist in the daylight."

Dallas stiffened at her words.

"Yeah, but it's extremely rare. Only old bloodlines have that ability. It's not passed through biting."

"But it is passed through birth," Rebel said, grinning to expose her fangs, which still looked fresh with blood, from a recent feeding.

And all at once Dallas knew without a doubt he was in danger.

Because the trojan horse was not some ghoul or random Djinn with no loyalty to Amora or The Heartsgrave.

It was Rebel.

Midnight's friend, the Djinn who he'd come to see as someone who annoyed the hell out of him, but who he sort of... liked. If only because she seemed to care about Midnight.

"You just couldn't stop digging, could you?" she said as she came closer.

Dallas stood defensively, readying to do all he could to take down this betrayer. He had no weapons, but that didn't mean he couldn't kill a monster like Rebel with his bare hands. He'd done it several times before.

"I don't know what you're talking about," he bit.

Rebel came up to Dallas, only a few inches away. She stared at him with fury, with *hate.*

"I must say, your little display of

intelligence surprised me. I almost worried you'd find me out. And maybe you would have, sooner, if you weren't so obsessed with Midnight's magical pussy." She sneered.

Dallas ground his jaw as he grabbed Rebel around the throat.

"Don't talk about my—"

"What, Dallas? What is she to you, hmm? Some piece of—"

"My *mate,*" he bit out, the word echoing with profound truth between them.

Rebel laughed maniacally.

"Does she know you sneak out to meet with other *hunters?* Hunters who will kill her if they find out what she is? Or what her daughter is?"

"Leave them out of this!" he roared as he tightened his grip.

Rebel spit in his face, causing only a second of distraction as he closed his eyes in response.

But it was all the distraction Rebel needed to slam Dallas up against a tree, her fangs poised near his neck as a *vampiric* hiss escaped her throat.

"You're a Djinn..." he uttered as he kicked at her.

But the strength she possessed was much more than he anticipated.

"No, sweetheart, I'm not. I just got all the pretty Djinn genes from my mama, but the vampire genes... well, that's all the Boracelli in me. And Boracelli's protect what belongs to them..." She closed her fingers around his throat, and he could feel his face flush as he struggled to breath.

"Then why don't you stop

monologuing and kill me?" he griped.

Rebel laughed as she licked his neck, the slimy texture making him recoil instantly. It wasn't the first time he'd been in this situation, but usually he could overpower a vampire. But Rebel wasn't a normal vampire.

She was a *hybrid*.

Like a Darkwing, but instead of vampire DNA muddled with demon blood, she was working with the strength of a strong old vampire bloodline, and Djinn strength. He was unfortunately, no match for her.

Yet somewhere in the struggle to breathe, he hung on to hope.

He would not go down without a fight, and he certainly would not go down without killing the fucking Boracelli who threatened to step in between him and his mate.

But he knew he could not fight this fight alone.

And so Dallas did the only thing he could think to do as he prepared for Rebel's bite. He reached out to his lifeline.

Find Malcolm Crowley.

He hoped Midnight would understand, given he couldn't explain in the course of a moment who Malcolm was or why he needed him, but Dallas knew without a doubt there was no one he trusted more to save his ass.

And he would be damned if Midnight tried to come to his rescue. He could not risk losing her, not now, not after...

Rebel's teeth sunk into his flesh and he cried out in agony, cursing her and everything to high hell. The sound of carnival music was faint in the forest air, as Dallas thought of Midnight, standing alone at the concessions, waiting for him.

He struggled against Rebel, who bit him on the other side of his neck, planting bites along his throat, but the searing pain of venom riddled his body, spreading like a wildfire and making it difficult to move. His limbs felt heavy, and his vision blurred.

"Mmmm, your wishful thinking is fucking delicious. You've got a lot of hope in there, don't you Viper?" she said wickedly.

Dallas opened his mouth to speak, but his throat felt as if it was closing up. His breaths came in hard as he struggled to breathe.

"I think you might be useful yet," she

purred.

Dallas tried to make his fingers move as she bit into the flesh above his collarbone, then his shoulder as she tore his shirt down. Venom spread throughout him without hesitation, and soon he felt as if his entire body was made of steel, as if he were forged in fire itself.

In his faded, blurred vision he saw another body come into the forest, a blur of black and purples but he couldn't make it out.

And the voice was unfamiliar as well, but the name Rebel spoke wasn't.

"Take him home, Trevor. I'll deal with his mate."

"It would be my pleasure, darling."

23

MAL WAITED FOR Dallas's signal, but it did not come. Which was highly unlike him.

Maybe being a monster really has changed him...

Mal slid his phone back in his pocket, focusing his attention on the woman in front of him, devouring the cotton candy he'd bought her.

Apparently, Cleo had never tried the

stuff, and he had to admit watching her excitement as she stuffed little puffs of pink sugar in her mouth was actually kind of... cute.

Though he wished she hadn't insisted on coming with him to the carnival. For one, Alaric had given him specific instructions to do exactly the opposite. He didn't know Alaric well—unless you counted the fact they both seemed to be mated to the same omega in a shocking twist of events—but he knew that the man was an alpha for a reason, and despite their coming together the other night—purely for Cleo—the man hated him as it was.

Directly defying the alpha's order was downright suicide for a wolf, no matter what pack they ran with.

Good thing I don't belong to any pack

and I'm not a fucking wolf.

"What's wrong?" she asked, her amber eyes softening.

"You've been staring at your phone for ten minutes," she said as she licked her lips, the sight causing Mal's cock to spring to attention.

What I wouldn't give to have those lips wrapped around my cock right now...

He cleared his throat.

"It's nothing," he said as he pushed the phone back in his pocket, feigning a smile.

"Just... old habits die hard, I guess," he lied.

Cleo raised an eyebrow.

"Mhmm. This wouldn't happen to have anything to do with your friend, would it? The one you're hunting?"

Mal froze at her words. Granted, his

mate knew he'd been hunting Dallas—which happened to coincide with the fact he was also hunting Cleo's... whatever the brother of your mate's *other* mate was, he hadn't told her he'd actually found Dallas. Mostly because he wasn't certain what the end of that story looked like.

Every part of Malcolm Crowley knew he should kill his former partner. No hunter would ever want to die, only to be brought back as the thing they hated, the thing they hunted.

It was a fate worse than death.

But when faced with his former partner in all his blue-eyed Djinn glory, Malcolm could not for the life of him find it in himself to do just that. And he hated that he couldn't. That in the face of everything they'd been through, he hesitated.

Then Dallas proposed an alliance, a job, as if nothing had changed despite the fact one of them feasted on mortals for a living now and one of them killed monsters who did such things.

"Maybe," Mal admitted. He found it hard to lie to the sweet omega who knew just how to infiltrate the walls he'd worked so hard to build.

She reached her hand across the table and grabbed his.

"You don't have to do this alone, you know," she said softly.

"I can help." Her eyes sparkled with truth and promise.

Mal ran his thumb over her knuckles as he set his other hand on top of hers. Even now, her touch stirred a hundred emotions, a heat in him he couldn't fight, and in her presence he didn't want to fight. He just wanted to fall into Cleo's warm arms, breathe her in, and let go. Which frightened him more than any threat of Djinn best friends.

Malcolm did not fall in love.

He couldn't afford to, with vengeance and blood curses taking up the majority of his life.

Is he really still my best friend, though?

"I know, my darling Clementine. But some things I just have to do on my own, you know?" he said. Just because Alaric had threatened him with bodily harm if he disobeyed him, didn't mean Mal wasn't going to do his own research. After all, Alaric didn't seem to be making any move at all to rescue his brother from the clutches of the bloodsuckers who'd taken him hostage.

He looked away from Cleo if only to refuse falling into her gaze, to avoid forgetting about the dangers at hand, and he laid his sight on two of the Djinn he'd seen at the last meeting at the Badlands. His shoulders tensed as a wave of panic surged through him as he noticed the one woman looked *drugged*.

Attacked, probably by those fucking bloodsuckers.

The bloodsuckers who wanted Cleo for their own Queen's fucked up science experiments and had wolf-napped the wrong werewolf.

And when it came to Clementine Srirocco, there was nothing Mal wouldn't do to make sure she stayed safe and untouched.

Instantly, he rose, heading in their

direction, Cleo wasting no time as she scarfed down the last bit of cotton candy, following him.

"Vampires?" he asked as he reached for the woman with blood seeping out of her neck, even though he already knew the answer.

The woman holding her, with a bright blue streak in her hair furrowed her eyebrows.

"Oh, yes, the poor thing! I'm afraid I might not have gotten there in time!" she said.

Mal shot her a look as he leaned forward to help carry the woman who was dead weight.

Her eyes fluttered.

Still conscious, that's good.

"They attacked first," he said as he looked at Cleo with alarm.

"I'm not—"

"Get out of here, Cleo. Go home. I'm not risking it. I can't risk them hurting you."

"We should retaliate," the woman said.

Cleo did not move.

"Clementine, this is not a discussion, I—"

"You seem to forget, Malcolm, that no one tells me what to do. Not anymore."

Mal pursed his lips.

Damnit Cleo, this is not the time to be stubborn!

"I'll take her from here," the woman said as she moved toward Mal.

"Thanks for the help, but..."

Something in Malcolm told him not to let go of the Djinn woman in his arms. A preternatural sense, deja vu, some weird bond shit he couldn't fathom at the moment.

He lifted the Djinn in his arms, her eyes fluttering as she tried to speak.

"I got her from here, I'll make sure she gets the attention she needs," he said as he nodded at Cleo.

"Go home, Cleo."

The black-haired woman with blue in her hair bit her lip, looking as if she wanted to argue.

Cleo's shoulders raised, a deep growl escaping her that made Mal's own hairs stand on edge.

"Stand your post. We'll inform Mayfield and make sure your friend is all right."

The woman glared back at her, looking between Mal and Cleo as if contemplating whether to fight back, to argue.

Cleo set her hand on Mal's shoulder, instantly feeding him a string of telepathic speak that he hadn't yet gotten used to. It was still quite weird to hear your mate in your head, nevertheless wrap ones head around the idea of a mate at all...

She's lying...

Mal turned to her, her golden gaze pleading with him.

I'm better with you than I am alone in some fucking tower, Mal. Let me help.

Malcolm grit his teeth.

Fucking hell, Cleo, Alaric is going to have my ass if something happens to you...

Mal took a step forward, as the other woman did.

"I'm sorry, I didn't catch your name,"

she said as Cleo closed the space between them, behind Mal.

Watching his back.

"It's Malcolm. Malcolm Crowley," he said.

"Malcolm..." the woman in his arms whispered.

His gaze flashed to her, her whisper shaky. It seemed as if speaking was difficult for her.

What did vampire venom do to other monsters?

He didn't even know. Perhaps this woman was already on her way to death in his arms...

"Dallas... needs you."

Malcolm's blood chilled like ice.

"How the fuck do you know Dallas..." he whispered as his heart picked up its pace. Her words lit a fire within him.

ARIEL DAWN

He's in trouble. Of course he is. Fuck! I should have known he wouldn't leave me in the dark like this without a damn reason... fucking asshole never thinks shit through...

"Mate," she whispered, the word disappearing in the air as she went limp.

"Fucking hell," Mal said as he held the woman a little closer. With that one word, Malcolm understood the power of that word, despite his own feelings.

Because he too had a mate he'd do anything for.

A glimmer of light in the darkness where the monsters lay, who set her hand on his shoulder, whose gaze found his, promising him peace he didn't deserve.

Jake Dallas had lost so much, but perhaps in the darkness, he found light, too.

And so Malcolm vowed as he ran across the fairgrounds with Dallas's *mate* in his arms, that Dallas was right.

Some bonds were stronger than blood, and some people were worth fighting for.

Malcolm, Cleo, Alaric, Midnight, & Dallas will return in Thorne Of Blood, Hunter Games Book #3!

Turn the page for a preview...

PREVIEW

"JUST A LITTLE harder," Rocky groaned. Cleo could see the sweat starting to form on his brow.

"I can't go any harder, Rocky," Cleo huffed as she collapsed against the tree.

"Yes, you can. You need to keep your strength up, or this heat will consume you."

Cleo pulled her knees to her chest, burying her face in her arms as she focused on trying to catch her breath. She was burning up, and it wasn't just because of her daily sprint with Rocky.

Nearly a year and a half ago she'd fallen into heat after arriving in Mahoning to live with the Thorne brothers, a strong, good pack in need of an omega like herself.

She'd gotten out of her childhood home in the nick of time, too; just in time to evade the vampires who'd attacked her town, who were searching for *her*.

An omega who hadn't fallen into heat yet.

Though the natural born enemies had always stayed away from her kind in an unspoken truce, it seemed there was one particular coven who was most interested in taking supernatural prisoners for their own gains; the Boracelli coven, fronted by a sadistic, twisted Queen who held no qualms about breaking unspoken bindings.

Though at the time, Cleo thought perhaps something had been wrong with her, for once she had arrived at the Thorne's estate, it seemed there was no heat. Day in and day out, she waited for a heat she thought would never come, wondering if somehow there had been a mistake, and what would her fate have been then if it was a mistake?

Would she be sent back home with her tail between her legs, a failure?

If she wasn't an omega, who would she have been?

Still, the truth and details surrounding her heat were murky at best, despite the fact she had fallen into it just as the seer had told her she would.

It will happen in Mahoning, the woman had said, and Cleo held onto that notion, even as the days droned on without one of the Thorne brothers doing so much as to rustle any sort of animal need in her.

And then suddenly, it *did* happen, but it wasn't the Thorne's who stirred her heat, despite the fact Rocky *insisted* to everyone in the pack, even his brothers, that it was him.

He knew the truth, after all—that Cleo's heat was stirred by a *human.*

A hunter, no less.

And that complicated everything. Though Cleo found herself growing more attracted to the Thornes by the day, she couldn't bring herself to cross the line with any of them.

Especially Sawyer.

Not when her mate, Malcolm Crowley, had *rejected* her, left her alone to wither away with the mad heat, in the privacy of her isolated quarters. Left her alone to hunger after a bond she wasn't certain she would ever finalize, despite how often she spoke with him on the phone, and even those moments were few and far between.

But a phone isn't the same as being with him in the flesh.

After Malcolm had left to hunt whatever it was that called him, Cleo had resigned herself to her quarters, mourning the human and his touch. The further away he was in the beginning, was downright sickening.

And then Alaric had disappeared

without so much as a goodbye, off on some urgent pack business that not even his brothers were privy to, taking with him the spark that had festered in her stomach, in her heart. The one that told her maybe, just maybe she could choose him... if she wanted.

Her room had gotten rather crowded from all the sweet, cozy omega gifts that arrived nearly daily from him in his absence, but they only made her feel worse.

Alaric had been upfront, though. He'd told her he would have given her everything, anything she wanted, if she would only ask.

But Clementine could not bring herself to ask Alaric for the one thing she wanted the most, because she knew not even the alpha of the pack could bring her to her moon; Malcolm Crowley.

Sawyer did not try to coax her out of her room, nor did he drop off gifts as his eldest brother had.

Instead, he'd only shown up to her room, drunk, nearly every night, begging for forgiveness before running his hands down her arm, or sliding his thick fingers in her hair, in a way that made her skin crawl.

Night after night, she refused Sawyer's advances, telling him to leave her be, shoving the man away, tossing him on his ass before locking her door to wallow once more that nothing would fix the hole in her heart. Everything was a stark reminder of what was missing.

Her only light in the darkness of the aftermath of Malcolm's rejection and Alaric's absence was Rocky Thorne.

Though to be fair, Rocky had been her ally since the day she arrived on the estate. Where his brothers hadn't been the gentlest of hostesses, treating Cleo as if she was a fragile doll or a *thing* to be kept, Rocky had offered her friendship, and alliance. He also happened to be the only one who knew the truth about who Malcolm was, and what had really transpired between them. He'd agreed in a heartbeat, no questions asked to protect Cleo and that truth, and not once did he push her or expect favors in return.

In fact, it was the opposite.

While Cleo fought her way through a multitude of stuffed animals and blankets, Rocky was the only one who did not try to soothe her aching soul. Instead, he looked at her with understanding and asked her to fight. Fight the heat, fight the desire to let the rejection pull her under, and Cleo relented.

She'd need to return to "normal" if only to placate the Thorne's who seemed to think her isolation was due to her pining for Alaric, and they'd only been a quarter correct. She *did* miss Alaric, but she missed much more than that. She missed her freedom, and Alaric was the key to it.

Who's off on official Alpha business because the pack always comes first...

She also needed to keep with the fabricated lie she and Rocky had spun, that he was the lucky Thorne who had stirred her heat. Eventually, she'd have to do something. She couldn't put off the instinct to mate forever.

She couldn't deny she felt something for the Thorne alpha, but she couldn't quite pinpoint what it was. It wasn't the same as what she felt for Malcolm, that she was certain of, but with as much as Alaric seemed to be off on "pack business" these days, the spark had dwindled to an annoying ember; not ready to die but not strong enough to ignite on its own without ample oxygen and attention.

Cleo had long heard that putting off "nature", fighting the mating bond itself, was damn near torture. Omegas were built to breed, after all.

It was natural, primal.

But Rocky had assured her she was strong enough to fight the heat until she'd made her decision. That despite what was *natural,* she still had a choice in the matter. She didn't have to give in so easily, if it wasn't what she wanted.

If they aren't what I want.

Training, fighting with Rocky had been the one thing in her endless days she'd found herself looking forward to, if only because it was the one time she could be free of the memory of Alaric's worried gaze every time he left, or Sawyer's lustful one every time she passed him in the hall.

With Rocky, Cleo could just... be.

She could be free, honest. With Rocky, she didn't have to hide or lie, and there was a beauty in that she couldn't deny, though she knew it was just who Rocky Thorne was.

He was caring, understanding, loyal, and most of all... he was comforting.

"Or I can just... give in. Stop fighting,"

she said as her breath caught in her throat.

Rocky sat down next to her, offering her a bottled water like an olive branch from the backpack they'd packed.

Cleo looked up from her spot in her lap.

Rocky shook the bottle, a hint of a smile tugging at his lips.

Like his older brothers, he held the same features; dark eyes and hair, tan, toned skin. But there was a light in his eyes that didn't exist in Sawyer's or even Alaric's.

Cleo's shoulders loosened as she unfurled herself like a flower, reaching out to take the bottle from his warm, long fingers. Her heart skipped a beat, the ice of the water bottle against her palm a welcome contrast to the heat that plagued her.

The touch of his fingertips against hers sent a shockwave through her body, directly to her groin, and she had to grind her teeth to keep the moan threatening to escape her throat at bay.

This is happening more frequently.

She brushed the feeling, the thoughts aside as she popped the cap and took a long, refreshing drink, practically swallowing down more than half in one gulp.

"Is that what you want? To give in?" Rocky asked, his voice even, devoid of any emotion one way or the other.

He was always like that with her, though. Where Alaric had difficulty showing his actual emotion, Sawyer seemed to not be able to think first before acting, Rocky was always ground zero. Neutral.

At that moment, as their eyes met, she understood by the briefest flicker, the shimmer of desire and hope that flashed in his eyes, that he was fighting just as hard as she was to remain neutral.

He was fighting, too, though she could not be sure what his beast of burden was.

"Sometimes I think it would be easier," she said as she licked her lips, which had already gone dry despite the cold drink.

The sun shone down on the two of them in the open field, which was miles away from the estate.

Out in the mountain forests, they could be free. Cleo loved it. The wind, the sun, the surrounding woods that felt more like home than the Thorne estate ever would.

As long as the vampires stayed at bay...

"To just let nature run its course, let the heat take over and just... mate."

"But?" He shot her a raised eyebrow.

Cleo drained the rest of her water, setting her hands in her lap. She looked to her side, taking in the sight of Rocky; of his toned, sweat slicked skin, his wet, dark hair hanging in his eyes. The sharp cut of his eyebrows, his jaw.

He truly was breathtaking for a young man.

"But my heart wants *him.* And I know it's dumb to wait for someone who might never come back, but..."

"You still want him. I know." Rocky's voice softened, his eyebrows furrowing as his gaze fell. His long lashes stood out against his skin, and he hung his head in defeat as he took his own sip of water.

Cleo sighed as the clouds moved in front of the sun, blocking the light. The air smelled like rain and earth, and she knew a storm was coming.

"We should head back," she said, wanting to make it home before it started pouring. She could always shift and run, but she hated doing so in stormy weather.

For starters, she didn't like the mud.

"Of course," he said, his breath catching in his throat. He shrugged off whatever was on his mind as he drained the last of his water bottle, discarding the empties in the backpack before zipping it up and tossing it on his back.

"Want to race back?" she asked,

wanting to dissolve the weird tension that had somehow formed between them.

"I thought you'd never ask," Rocky said with a grin as Cleo rose.

"On the count of three," she said.

The clouds moved in, and just as Cleo counted three, the rain came, and as she ran through the rain, Rocky Thorne beside her, keeping her pace, she closed her eyes and let the water wash away all thoughts of hunters and alphas. Instead, she focused on the beta beside her, chasing her to the edge of the estate like he longed to catch her, and her heart beat faster.

Because for a startling moment, Cleo wished to be caught.

BLOOD OF THE LOST

Follow Ariel Dawn to keep up to date on
the release date for Thorne of Blood!
http://www.ariel-dawn.com/

OTHER BOOKS BY ARIEL DAWN

The Hunter Games

Blood Of My Enemy

Blood Of The Lost

Thorne Of Blood

Speed Dating with the Denizens of the Underworld Series

Hecate

Hades

Orion

Athena

Spike

The Forevermore Series

In The Cards

In The Blood

In The Shadows

BLOOD OF THE LOST

In The Deep

In The Garden

In The Night

Shifters Of Starfall Creek Series

Hollow's Sunrise

Hollow's Sunset

Hollow's Legacy

Shifters of Starfall Creek Collection:

Books 1-3

Sign up for Ariel Dawn's newsletter and

claim your sweet treat!

https://mailchi.mp/e5f326e433bf/dawn

-breaks-official-newsletter

CONNECT WITH ARIEL DAWN

Website

http://www.ariel-dawn.com/

Goodreads:

http://www.goodreads.com/authorariel
dawn

Bookbub:

http://www.bookbub.com/authors/ariel
-dawn

Facebook:

http://www.facebook.com/authorarielda
wn

Twitter:

https://twitter.com/ArielDawn10

Join Dusk Chasers—Ariel Dawn's Official Readers Group for access to exclusive content!

ABOUT ARIEL DAWN

USA TODAY BESTSELLING AUTHOR Ariel Dawn grew up as an avid reader and is a creative soul.

What started out as writing reviews for indie romance authors led to featuring quirky, stereotypical, and weird covers on her Instagram Wrong Turn Romance, which gave her the courage to finally decide to live her dream and become an author.

Ariel writes plot driven paranormal romance and hopes to venture into fantasy and rom-com in the future. When she isn't writing, she can be found cosplaying, attending conventions, creating all sorts of artwork in her studio, or editing photos for her photography business.

A self-professed geek and foodie, she loves hanging out with family and friends and playing video games and board games with her retro gamer husband.